EX LIBRIS

VINTAGE **CLASSICS**

H. E. BATES

H. E. Bates was born in Northamptonshire in 1905. He published his first novel, *The Two Sisters*, when he was twenty, and for the next decade built up a reputation as a writer of great versatility. During the Second World War, Bates was commissioned by the RAF as a short story writer, and he wrote the acclaimed collections *How Sleep the Brave* and *The Greatest People in the World*. His most popular creation was the effervescent Larkin family about whom he wrote five novels, including *The Darling Buds of May* and *A Little of What You Fancy*. In 1973 H. E. Bates was awarded the CBE. He died in 1974.

OTHER WORKS BY H. E. BATES

Novels

Fair Stood the Wind for France
The Cruise of the Breadwinner
The Purple Plain
Love for Lydia
The Nature of Love
The Sleepless Moon
The Darling Buds of May
A Breath of French Air
When the Green Woods Laugh
Oh! To be in England
A Little of What You Fancy
A Moment in Time

Short Stories

Day's End and Other Stories
The Woman Who Had Imagination
The Wedding Party
My Uncle Silas

Essays

Down The River
The Happy Countryman
In the Heart of the Country

H. E. BATES

How Sleep the Brave

Brave

THE COMPLETE STORIES OF FLYING OFFICER 'X'

VINTAGE

7 9 10 8 6

Vintage
20 Vauxhall Bridge Road,
London SW1V 2SA

Vintage Classics is part of the Penguin Random House
group of companies whose addresses can be found at
global.penguinrandomhouse.com

Penguin
Random House
UK

First published in Great Britain by Jonathan Cape in 1952

A CIP catalogue record for this book is available from the
British Library

ISBN 9780099442035

Printed and bound by Clays Ltd, St Ives plc

Penguin Random House is committed to a sustainable future
for our business, our readers and our planet. This book is made
from Forest Stewardship Council® certified paper.

MIX
Paper | Supporting
responsible forestry
FSC® C018179

CONTENTS

AUTHOR'S NOTE

The original volumes of the *Flying Officer 'X'* stories, *The Greatest People in the World* and *How Sleep the Brave*, were dedicated to the late Hilary St. George Saunders, from whose enthusiasm and vision the entire project of writing them derived so much; and to John Pudney, whose friendly watchfulness and greater experience in practical Air Force matters saved both them and myself from various pitfalls. Although three new stories have been added to the present collection time has shown no reason why the names of these two friends should not remain coupled on the dedication page. Indeed the untimely death of Hilary St. George Saunders only provides another opportunity of paying homage to a man who was so much concerned, both in enthusiasm and affection, with these stories and their genesis.

THERE'S NO FUTURE IN IT

THE NIGHTS HE was not flying they would drive back late to the station, using her car. The flare-path would be laid; the lights on the hangars would shine like red stars in the winter darkness about the flat land. Sometimes the searchlights would be up, throwing a blue-white fire that fell widely like moonlight on the dark trees and hedges and on the winding road. They would sit in the car and, holding each other, talk for a long time. Frost on the very coldest nights would form like a silver collar on the glass of the windscreen and sometimes, on very still nights, he would wind down the window of the car and listen for a moment or two to the silence outside. She would lean her head on his shoulder and look upwards into the dark sky and then, listening too, hear the sound of the bombers coming home.

It did not seem to matter much that they were never likely to be married. He was rather small and compact, with fresh grey eyes that he sometimes did not seem able to focus correctly. He had thirty-one operational trips to his credit and all that seemed to matter was that he should continue coming back.

The morning afterwards, perhaps, he would ring the office. He would say simply, 'Hullo, dear, tonight'. She would try to remain calm, and later, perhaps, if operations were scrubbed, he would ring her again and she would find herself trembling as she put down the telephone, all her pretence of calmness gone.

She knew generally that he would be briefed in the early afternoon. He would take off about three o'clock or a little later and, according to the target, come back somewhere between eight and ten. It would often be too late to ring her after interrogation, but going to bed she would try to lie awake for the sound of the telephone. Sometimes she would fall asleep with the light still burning and would wake up in the small hours of the morning, bewildered and startled, not knowing where she was. Twice she fell half-asleep and did not hear the telephone. Downstairs her father heard it, but after answering it, did not come to tell her who it was.

Her father was a rather big, grey-haired man with cheeks like loose pink rubber. He rolled his own cigarettes and it seemed to her that she never saw him without a newspaper. He rolled the cigarettes very badly – the tobacco fell wastefully on his clothes. The war had developed in him the latent qualities of the amateur strategist, and he always discussed the war while waving an untidy, wasteful cigarette. 'We ought to have cut the Tripoli road long ago. Long ago. You have only to look at the map. The same with the bombing of Berlin. What's gone wrong? Why aren't we over there more? Why aren't we over there night after night? Striking early and often is the decisive factor. You'd suppose it wouldn't escape our people.'

'Perhaps it's the weather,' she would say.

'Weather? There's another thing that beats me. Argue on simple lines, draw some absolutely logical conclusion which ought to be apparent to the merest child, and you always get the same answer. The weather! I don't doubt the weather is sometimes bad. But far from always, far from always. It's too often a convenient excuse – like the workman blaming his tools.'

'Nevertheless it nearly always is the weather.'

'Oh? Then what about last night? Clear moonlight like day. And was there a single operation? A couple of bombers over Brest.'

'You talk as if Brest were a seaside resort.'

'Look at the weather again tonight. Magnificent. And in the morning what shall we hear? The same old story again, I suppose. A handful of bombers over Brest. Or nothing at all.'

'It's probably the most heavily defended place in Europe,' she said. 'It's just plain hell.'

'Kitty, Kitty,' her mother said. She looked up from her knitting, always khaki, and looked down again.

'Also I think you may find that tonight has been a big thing.'

'Oh! you know, do you?'

'No. Not exactly. I've an idea, that's all.'

'Ah! Your pilot friend.'

She did not speak.

'You haven't brought him in lately.'

'No, dear,' her mother said.

'They spend most of their time out,' her father said. 'Somewhere.'

Her mother spoke without looking up from her knitting.

'Were you at the Red Lion last week?' her mother said. 'We heard you were there. Drinking with Air Force officers.'

'I was.'

'Is that the kind of place to be?' her father said.

'Drinking,' her mother said. 'It's not nice. Do you think so?'

'I want to be wherever he is.'

'Even there? Couldn't you give him up?' her mother said. 'He struck me as being older than he said. Do you know much

3

about him? You are only twenty. It's all so terribly unsure. Perhaps he is married. Do you know?'

She did not answer.

'He looks older than twenty-four,' her mother said. 'Experienced. His eyes look old.'

She got up, calmly enraged, definite. 'He has done things that make him old,' she said, and went out of the room.

The following night they drove back late to the station. With the moon rising and the searchlights up, the road shone misty white between the dark hedges. The evening lay behind them, as always, simply secure; a few rounds of light ale at the Red Lion, the boys coming in group by group, the rounds growing, the crews mixing, sergeants with squadron leaders, gunners with navigators, warm broad Canadian voices mingled with English; and then the drive home, the blue lighting of the searchlights, and the moonlight throwing into relief the black winter trees, the hangars lit by red stars, the huge solitary dispersed aircraft in the fields; and lastly the silence after the car had stopped beyond the gate of the station.

'Was it a good trip, darling?'

He did not answer.

'Bad?'

'Pretty bad.'

'Did you have trouble?'

'The usual. Ten-tenths most of the way and then some hellish flak.'

She thought of her father. She saw him in an armchair, rolling the cigarettes, waving a newspaper. 'Always the weather!'

'I'm sorry I couldn't ring,' he said. 'It was late when we got in for interrogation. I didn't want to wake you.'

'I was awake,' she said.

They sat still, not speaking. She thought again of her father.

'Tell me about the trip.'

'Nothing to tell. Routine stuff.'

She did not like the sound of his voice, tired and guarded; the feeling that part of him was deliberately withheld.

'I can tell when you have trouble.'

'What trouble? No trouble at all.'

'Why have you got your hand in your pocket?' she said. 'You're had it there all the time.'

'All right,' he said.

He began suddenly to tell her something about the trip. Though she had heard so much of it before, the awful significance of it was not lessened. He told her about the weather; ten-tenths, a bad storm soon after they turned for home, a spot of ice. 'They put up a hell's own flak at us. Just routine stuff, only a bloody sight worse. And they hit my hand. Took the skin off, that's all.' He kept it in his pocket.

She knew that he was not telling everything, that he never did, perhaps never would. Routine stuff, hellish flak, a spot of ice; the same words, the same repeated demand on courage, on fear if you like, the same holding back. She thought once more of her father: the world of the newspaper, the protest, the old indignations. To contrast it with the world of flak and ice, the long darkness of endurance, the spell of cold and strain thirty-one times repeated, was so difficult and angrily confusing that she said only, 'Does your hand hurt? Can I do anything for you?'

'Thanks, darling. I'm O.K.'

She remembered something.

'What time did interrogation finish? Why were you so late?'

'It wasn't so late. Not so very late.'

'If it wasn't so late why didn't you ring me?'

'I didn't want to wake you.'

'Tell me what happened,' she said.

He looked beyond the car window and said, 'We got a bit shot up. Just one of those things.'

'Bad?'

'Bad enough. A lump of flak blew a hole as big as a cartwheel in the starboard wing and the transmitter was u.s. Shaky landing. But why pick on me? It happens every day.'

'Not to you.'

'It happens,' he said.

'You hate it, don't you?' she said.

'Hate what?' he said.

'You hate going, don't you, time after time? The same place. The same job. The same everything. I know you hate it.'

'I hate it like hell,' he said. He looked beyond the car window again. The diffused lighting of the searchlights and the cloudy moon shone on the misted windscreen. The trees were black against it. 'But I hate what they're doing even more. That's what I really hate. What they do to me isn't half of what I mean doing to them. Not half. Not a quarter. Not a hundredth part. Is there anything wrong about hatred?'

She was thinking of her father, fussy with indignation, and she did not answer.

'It's good honest downright emotion, isn't it?' he said.

'Yes.'

'Sometimes I think we want more of it,' he said. 'God, sometimes I think we do.'

When at last she drove back from the station it was later than she thought. But at the house, to her surprise, her father and mother were still up. Her mother looked up from her knitting and her father looked at his watch.

'Either my watch is fast or it's ten past twelve.'

She did not speak.

'Even the Red Lion closes at ten.'

'It so happens I haven't been there.'

Her father coughed heavily. 'Does your pilot friend realize that we sit here, waiting?'

She did not answer.

'We have a right to be considered.'

She stood slowly taking off her gloves.

'You'll agree that he owes us something, won't you?'

She stood thinking of the long flight in the darkness, the hellish flak, the hole in the wing, the shell through the fuselage, the shaky landing; routine stuff; easy, nothing to tell, something done again and again. Her mind became unsteady with hatred. She looked at her mother. The clean prejudiced hands were motionless on the knitting. Her father with the evening newspaper folded between his fingers stood with his back to the dying fire.

'Is he married?' her mother said.

'Does it matter?' she said.

Her father crackled the newspaper.

'My dear child, my dear child! Does it matter? I ask you. What about the future? Is there any future in that?'

'No,' she said; 'there's no future in it.'

She wanted to go on speaking, but her thoughts were disrupted and dispersed in the corners of her mind and she could not gather them together. She wanted to say why there was no future. She wanted to tell them about the flak, the darkness, and the bitter cold, about the way the tracer bullets came in at you so slowly that you could watch them until suddenly they hurled with red frenzy past your face, about the hatred and the monotony and the courage that was greater because it was rarefied by terror. She wanted to tell them that if there was any future it lay through this.

She went out of the room and went upstairs instead. She felt stifled by the warmth of the room downstairs and, not putting on the light, she opened the window and stood looking out. The air was bright with frost and the coldness struck with a momentary shock on her face and hands.

She stood there for a long time, looking out. The moon was going down beyond the houses. The searchlights were no longer up beyond the town. The sky was clear and calm and, as if there were no war and as it might be in the future, if there were a future, there was no sound of wings.

THE YOUNG MAN FROM
KALGOORLIE

I

HE LIVED WITH his parents on a sheep-farm two hundred miles north-east of Kalgoorlie. The house was in the old style; a simple white wooden cabin to which a few extensions had been added by successive generations. On the low hills east of the farm there were a few eucalyptus trees; his mother grew pink and mauve asters under the house windows in summer; and in spring the wattle was in blossom everywhere, like lemon foam. All of his life had been lived there, and the war itself was a year old before he knew that it had even begun.

On the bomber station, surrounded by flat grey English hills cropped mostly by sugar-beet and potatoes and steeped in winter-time in thick windless fogs that kept the aircraft grounded for days at a time, he used to tell me how it had come to happen that he did not know the war had started. It seemed that he used to go down to Kalgoorlie only once, perhaps twice, a year. I do not know what sort of place Kalgoorlie is, but it seemed that he did there, on that one visit or so, all the things that anyone can do on a visit to almost any town in the world. He used to take a room for a week at a hotel, get up at what he thought was a late hour every morning – about eight o'clock – and spend most of the day

9

looking at shops, eating, and then looking at shops again. In the evenings he used to take in a cinema, eat another meal, have a couple of glasses of beer in the hotel lounge and then go to bed. He confessed that it wasn't very exciting and often he was relieved to get back into the Ford and drive steadily back to the sheep-farm and the familiar horizon of eucalyptus trees, which after the streets of Kalgoorlie did not seem a bad prospect at all. The truth was that he did not know anyone in Kalgoorlie except an aunt, his mother's sister, who was very deaf and used a patent electrical acoustic device which always seemed to go wrong whenever he was there and which he had once spent more than a day trying to repair. He was very quiet and he did not easily get mixed up with people; he was never drunk and more than half the time he was worried that his father was making a mess of things at home.

It was this which was really the cause of his not knowing about the war. His father was an unimaginative and rather careless man to whom sheep were simply sheep and grass simply grass and who had kept sheep on the same two thousand acres, within sight of the same eucalyptus trees, for thirty years, and expected to go on keeping them there for the rest of his life. He did not understand that two years of bad luck had anything to do with his having kept sheep in the same way, on the same grass, for so long. It was the son who discovered that. He began to see that the native grasses were played out, and in their place he decided to make sowings of Italian rye-grass and subterranean clover; and soon he was able to change the flocks from one kind of grass to another and then on to a third and soon he could see an improvement in the health of every breed they had.

After that he was virtually in charge of the farm. His parents, who had always thought him a wonderful person, now thought him more wonderful still. When neighbours came – and this too was not often, since the nearest farm was another thirty miles up country – they talked of nothing but Albert's achievement. The sheep had improved in health, the yield of wool had increased, and even the mutton, they argued, tasted sweeter now, more like the meat of thirty years ago. 'Got a proper old-fashioned flavour,' his mother said.

It was about a year after these experiments of his – none of them very original, since he had simply read up the whole subject in an agricultural paper – that war broke out. It seemed, as he afterwards found out, that his mother first heard of it on an early morning news bulletin on the radio. She was scared and she called his father. The son himself was out on the farm, riding round on horseback taking a look at the sheep before breakfast. When he came in to breakfast he switched on the radio, but nothing happened. He opened up the radio and took a look at it. All the valves were warm, but the detector valve and another were not operating. It seemed a little odd but he did not take much notice of it. All he could do was to write to Kalgoorlie for the spare valves, and he did so in a letter which he wrote after dinner that day. It was three miles to the post-box and if there were any letters to be posted his mother took them down in the afternoon. His mother took this letter that afternoon and tore it up in little pieces.

That must have happened, he discovered, to every letter he wrote to the Kalgoorlie radio shop in the next twelve months. No valves ever came and gradually, since it was summer and sheep-shearing time and the busiest season of the year, the family got used to being without the radio. His father and mother said they even preferred it. All the time he had no idea of the things they were doing in order to keep the war from him. The incoming post arrived once a week and if there were any letters for him his mother steamed them open, read them and then put the dangerous ones away in a drawer upstairs.

The newspapers stopped coming, and when he remarked on it his father said he was tired of wasting good money on papers that were anyway nearly a week old before they came. If there were visitors his mother managed to meet them before they reached the house. In October the sheep-shearing contractors came and his father, ordinarily a rather careful man, gave every man an extra pound to keep his mouth shut. All through that summer and the following winter his mother looked very ill, but it was not until later that he knew the reason of it – the strain of intercepting the letters, of constantly guarded conversation, of warning neighbours and callers, of making excuses and even of lying to him, day after day, for almost a year.

The time came when he decided to go to Kalgoorlie. He always went there about the same time of the year, in late August, before the busy season started. His parents must have anticipated and dreaded that moment, and his father did an amazing thing. In the third week of August, early one morning, he put two tablespoonfuls of salt in a cup of hot tea and drank it, making himself very sick. By the time Albert came in to breakfast his father was back in bed, very yellow in the face, and his mother was crying because he had been taken suddenly ill. It was the strangest piece of deception of all and it might have succeeded if his father had not overdone things. He decided to remain in bed for a second week, making himself sick every third or fourth day, knowing that once September had come Albert would never leave. But Albert was worried. He did not like the recurrent sickness which now affected his father and he began to fear some sort of internal trouble.

'I'm going to Kalgoorlie whether you like it or not,' he said, 'to get a doctor.'

II

It was on the bomber station, when he had become a pilot, that he used to tell me of that very first day in Kalgoorlie, one of the most remarkable in his life. When he left the farm his mother seemed very upset, and began crying. He felt that she was worried about his father; he was increasingly worried too and promised to be back within three days. Then he drove down to Kalgoorlie alone: perhaps the only man in Australia who did not know that the war was a year old.

He arrived at Kalgoorlie about four o'clock in the afternoon and the town seemed much the same as ever. He drove straight to the hotel he always stayed at, booked himself a room and went upstairs to wash and change. About five o'clock he came down again and went into the hotel lounge for a cup of tea. Except for a word or two with the cashier and the lift-boy he did not speak to a soul. He finished his tea and then decided to go to the downstairs saloon, as he always did, to get himself a haircut. There were several people waiting in the saloon, but he decided to wait too. He sat down and picked up a paper.

He must have gone on staring at that paper, not really reading it, for about ten minutes. It was late August and the Nazis were bombing London. He did not understand any of it; who was fighting or what were the causes of it. He simply took in, from the headlines, the story of the great sky battles, the bombing, the murder and destruction, as if they were part of a ghastly fantasy. For the moment he did not feel angry or sick or outraged because he had been deceived. He got up and went out into the street. What he felt, he told me, was very much as if you were suddenly to discover that you had been living in a house where, without knowing it, there was a carrier of smallpox. For months you have lived an ordinary tranquil life, unsuspecting and unafraid, and then suddenly you made the awful discovery that every fragment of your life, from the dust in your shoes to the air you breathed, was contaminated and that you had been living in danger. Because you knew nothing you were not afraid; but the moment you knew anything all the fears and terrors you had not felt in the past were precipitated into a single terrible moment of realization.

He also felt a fool. He walked up and down the street. As he passed shops, read placards, saw men in service uniform, fragmentary parts of his life during the past year became joined together, making sense: the broken radio, his unanswered letters, the newspapers, his mother's nervousness and the fact, above all, that they had not wanted him to come to Kalgoorlie. Slowly he understood all this. He tried to look on it as the simple cunning of country people. He was still too confused to be angry. But what he still did not understand, and what he had to find out about soon, was the war. He did not even know how long it had been going on. He stopped on a street-corner and bought another newspaper. The day before, he read, eighty-seven aircraft had been shot down over England. His hands were trembling as he read it, but it did not tell him the things he wanted to know. And he realized suddenly, as he stood there trembling in the hot sunshine, so amazed that he was still without feeling, that there was no means of knowing these things. He certainly could not know by asking. He imagined for a moment the effect of asking anyone, in the street, or the hotel, or back in the barber's saloon, a simple question like 'Can you tell me when the war began?' He felt greatly oppressed by a sense of ridicule and bewilderment, by the fear that now, any time he opened his mouth, he was likely to make a ghastly fool of himself.

He walked about for an hour or more, pretending to look

at shops, before it occurred to him what to do. Then it came to him quite suddenly that he would go and see the only other person he knew, who, like himself, could be cut off from the world of reality; the deaf aunt who lived in Kalgoorlie.

So he spent most of that evening in the old-fashioned parlour of her house, drinking tea, eating custard tarts, lightly brown with veins of nutmeg, and talking as steadily as he could into the electrical acoustic device fixed to the bodice of her dress. From such remarks as 'Things look pretty tough in England. Let's see, how long exactly has it been going on now?' he learned most of the elementary things he wanted to know. But there were still things he could not ask simply because he had no knowledge of them. He could not ask about France or Poland or Holland or Norway. All that he really understood clearly was that England and Germany were at war; that England was being bombed every day by great forces of aircraft; that soon, perhaps, she would be invaded. The simplicity and limitation of his knowledge was in a way, as he said, a good thing. For as he ate the last of the old lady's custard tarts and drank the last cup of tea and said good night to her he changed from being the man who knew least about the war in all Australia to the man who had perhaps the clearest, simplest, and most vivid conception of it in the whole continent. Forty years back his father and mother had emigrated from Lincolnshire to Kalgoorlie. Young, newly wed, and with about eighty pounds apart from their passage money, they started a new life. Now the roots of their existence, and so in a way the roots of his own existence, were being threatened with annihilation. This was the clear, simple terrible thing he understood in such a clear, simple, terrible way.

When he got back to his hotel he drafted a telegram to his parents, telling them, as well as he could, that he understood.

Then in the morning he went round to the nearest recruiting centre. I have not so far described what he was like. He was rather tall, fair, and brown in the face; his eyes were a cool blue and his lips thin, determined, and rather tight. He was just twenty-two and he had no way of holding back his anger.

'I want to be a pilot,' he said.

'All right,' they said. 'Good. But you can't be a pilot all of a sudden, just like that.'

'No?' he said. 'No? We'll bloody soon see.'

III

He adjusted himself as time went on but he carried some of his first angry, clear, terrible conceptions of things across the sea; across the Pacific to Vancouver, across the Atlantic to England. He was never angry with his parents and they in turn ceased being afraid about him. He used to describe to me how he went home on his first leave. From being stupidly affectionate in one way about him they became stupidly affectionate in quite another. They had not wanted him to go; now, because he had gone, they behaved as if they had everything to do with sending him and nothing to do with keeping him away. They had arranged a party and he said it was the largest gathering of folks anyone had ever seen on the farm. They invited everyone for thirty miles around and one or two people from fifty miles away. They killed several spring lambs and about fifteen fowls and tea was brewing all day long. At night they sang hymns and old songs in the drawing-room round the piano, and they slept in round beds on the floor. In the end he was almost glad to get away.

He promised to write to them often, and he promised also to keep a diary. He always did write and he always kept the diary. He sailed for Vancouver early in the year and by the spring he was flying Ansons and by the summer he was in England. It was an uncertain and rather treacherous summer and the harvest was wet and late in the corn country where we were. The potato fields were blighted, so that they looked as if spattered by drops of coffee on the dark rainy autumn days, and for long periods low cloud kept the aircraft down. Gradually the harvest fields were cleaned and the potatoes sacked and carted away, and in place of them you could see pale golden cones of sugar-beet piled in the fields and by the roadsides. I mention the weather because it was almost the only thing about England that troubled him. He longed for the hot dry air of the Australian summer and he used to tell me, as we gazed over the wet flat country, of the days when he had flown over Victoria in a Moth in his shirt sleeves and had looked down on the white beaches shining all along the coast in the sun.

The weather troubled him because his anger was still there. He felt that it frustrated him. He could never forget the day in Kalgoorlie when he had first read of the bombing and the mass murder in England and the very headlines of the paper had seemed like an awful dream. He felt that so much of his life had still to be brought up to date. Something had to be vindicated. Yet you could never tell that he was angry. It was easier to tell that he was sometimes afraid: not that he was afraid of dying or being hurt, but of some material thing like mishandling a kite. As he graduated from Moths to Ansons, to Blenheims and Wellingtons, and finally to Stirlings, he felt each time that he would never be big enough for the change to the bigger aircraft, yet it was always because of that fear that he was big enough.

Late that autumn he became captain of a Stirling and about the same time he got to know a girl. Two or three evenings a week, if there were no operations, we used to go down into the town and drink a few glasses of beer at a pub called the Grenadier, and one evening this girl came in. She was very dark and rather sophisticated, with very red lips, and she never wore her coat in the ordinary way but simply had it slung on her shoulders, with the sleeves empty and dangling. 'This is Olivia,' he said. For some reason I never knew her other name; we most often called her Albert's popsie, but after that, every night we were in the Grenadier, she would come in and soon, after talking for a time, they would go off somewhere alone together. The weather was very bad at that time and he saw her quite often. And then for a few nights it cleared and one night, before going over to Bremen, he asked if I would keep his date with her and make his apologies and explain.

He had arranged to see her at seven o'clock and I made a bad impression by being late. She was irritable because I was late and because, above all, I was the wrong person.

'Don't be angry,' I said. 'I'm very sorry.'

'I'm not angry,' she said. 'Don't think it. I'm just worried.'

'You needn't be worried,' I said.

'Why not? Aren't you worried? You're his friend.'

'No, I'm not worried,' I said. 'I'm not worried because I know what sort of pilot he is.'

'Oh! you do, do you? Well, what sort of pilot is he?' she said. 'He never tells me. He never talks about it at all.'

'They never do,' I said.

'Sometimes I think I'll never know what sort of person he is at all. Never!'

I felt there was little I could say to her. She was angry because I was the wrong person and because she was frustrated. I brought her several drinks. For a time she was quieter and then once more she got excited.

18

'One night he'll get shot down and about all I'll know of him is that his name was Albert!'

'Take it easy,' I said. 'In the first place he won't get shot down.'

'No? How are you so sure?'

'Because he's the sort that shoots other people down first.'

'Are you trying to be funny?' she said.

'No,' I said; and for a few minutes I tried to tell her why it was not funny and why I had spoken that way. I tried quite hard but I do not think she understood. I realized that she knew nothing of all that had happened in Kalgoorlie; the blank year, the awful discovery about England, the bewilderment and the anger. I tried to make her see that there is a type that thinks of nothing but the idea that he may be shot at; and that there is another type, of which he was one, which thinks of nothing but shooting first. 'He's glad to go. He wants to go. It's what he lives for,' I said. 'Don't you see?'

No sooner had I said it than I realized that it was the stupidest thing in the world to say. It was herself, not flying, that she wanted him to live for. She did not understand, and it would have sounded very silly if I had tried to tell her, that he was engaged on something like a mission of vengeance, that because of all that had happened in Kalgoorlie, and especially that one day in Kalgoorlie, he felt that he had something damnable and cruel and hideous to wipe out from his conception of what was a decent life on earth. Every time he went up something was vindicated. Nor did she understand, and again it might have sounded foolish too, that it was the living and positive clarity of the whole idea that was really his preservation. All I could say was, 'He's the sort that goes on coming back and coming back until they're fed up with him and make him an instructor.'

Nevertheless, that night, her fears were almost justified.

The flak over Bremen was very hostile and it seemed that he had to take a lot of hasty evasive action before he could get clear away along the coast. They had brought him down even then to about two thousand feet. The searchlights were very thick too and it was like daylight in the aircraft marking the time. But as if he couldn't possibly miss the opportunity, he came down to three hundred feet, roaring over the searchlight batteries as his gunners attacked them. They flew for about forty miles in this way, until finally something hit the outer starboard engine and holed the starboard wing. After that they were in a very bad way and got home, as he said, later than originally proposed.

I do not think he told her about this. It went down into his log and some of it may have gone down into the diary he had promised faithfully to keep for his people back on the farm. He was satisfied that he had blown out about twenty searchlights and that was all. Something else was vindicated. Two days later he had another go. In quite a short daylight attack along the Dutch coast he got into an argument with a flak ship. He was in a very positive mood and he decided to go down to attack. As he was coming in, his rear-gunner sighted a formation of Messerschmitts coming up astern, and two minutes later they attacked him. He must have engaged them for about fifteen minutes. He had always hated Messerschmitts and to be attacked by them made him very angry indeed. At the end of the engagement he had shot down two of them and had crippled a third, but they in turn had holed the aircraft in fifteen places. Nevertheless he went down just to carry out his instruction of giving the flak ship a good-bye kiss. She had ceased firing and he went in almost to low level and just missed her with his last two bombs by the stern. As he was coming home his outer port engine gave up, but he tootled in just before darkness, quite happy. 'A piece o' cake,' he said.

I know that he did not tell her about this either, and I could see that she had some excuse for thinking him undemonstrative and perhaps unheroic. For the next two days there was thick fog and rime frost in the early morning that covered the wings of the Stirlings with dusty silver. He was impatient because of the fog and we played many games of cribbage in the mess on the second day, while the crews were standing down.

On the third day he came back from briefing with a very satisfied look on his face. 'A little visit to Mr. Salmon and Mr. Gluckstein at Brest,' he said. He had been flying just a year. He had done twenty trips, all of them with the same meaning. It was a bright calm day, without cloud, quite warm in the winter sun. There were pools of water here and there on the runways and looking through the glasses I could see little brushy silver tails spurting up from the wheels of the aircraft as they taxied away.

When I looked into the air, again through the glasses, I saw two aircraft circling round, waiting to formate before setting course. One of them was smoking a little from the outer port engine. The smoking seemed to increase a little and then become black. Suddenly it seemed as if the whole engine burst silently and softly into crimson flower. I kept looking through the glasses, transfixed, but suddenly the aircraft went away behind the hangars as it came down.

That evening I waited until it was quite dark before going into the town. I went into the bar of the Grenadier and the girl was standing by the bar talking to the barmaid. She was drinking a port while waiting for him to come.

'Hullo,' she said. Her voice was cold and I knew that she was disappointed.

'Hullo. Could you come outside a moment?' I said.

She finished her port and came outside and we stood in the

street, in the darkness. Some people went by, shining a torch on the dirty road, and in the light I could see the sleeves of her coat hanging loose, as if she had no arms. I waited until the people had gone by, and then, not knowing how to say it, I told her what had happened. 'It wasn't very heroic,' I said. 'It was damnable luck. Just damnable luck, that's all.'

I was afraid she would cry.

She stood still and quite silent. I felt that I had to do something to comfort her and I made as if to take hold of her arm, but I only caught the sleeve, which was dead and empty. I felt suddenly far away from her and as if we had known two different people: almost as if she had not known him at all.

'I'll take you to have a drink,' I said.

'No.'

'You'll feel better.'

'Why did it have to happen?' she said suddenly, raising her voice. 'Why did it have to happen?'

'It's the way it often does happen,' I said.

'Yes, it's the way it often does happen!' she said. 'Is that all you care? Is that all anyone cares? It's the way it happens!'

I did not speak. For a moment I was not thinking of her. I was thinking of a young man in a barber's saloon in Kalgoorlie, about to make the shocking discovery that the world was at war and that he did not know it.

'Yes, it's the way it happens!' she said. I could not see her face in the darkness, but her voice was very bitter now. 'In a week nobody will ever know he flew. He's just one of thousands who go up and never come back. I never knew him. Nobody ever knew him. In a week nobody will know him from anyone else. Nobody will even remember him.'

For a moment I did not answer. Now I was not thinking of him. I was thinking of the two people who had so bravely and stupidly kept the war from him and then had so bravely and proudly let him go. I was thinking of the farm with the sheep and the eucalyptus trees, the pink and mauve asters and the yellow spring wattle flaming in the sun. I was thinking of the thousands of farms like it, peopled by thousands of people like them: the simple, decent, kindly, immemorial people all over the earth.

'No,' I said to her. 'There will be many who will remember him.'

It's Just the Way It Is

NOVEMBER RAIN FALLS harshly on the clean tarmac, and the wind, turning suddenly, lifts sprays of yellow elm leaves over the black hangars.

The man and woman, escorted by a sergeant, look very small as they walk by the huge cavernous openings where the bombers are.

The man, who is perhaps fifty and wears a black overcoat and bowler hat, holds an umbrella slantwise over the woman, who is about the same age, but very grey and slow on her feet, so that she is always a pace or two behind the umbrella and must bend her face against the rain.

On the open track beyond the hangars they are caught up by the wind, and are partially blown along, huddled together. Now and then the man looks up at the Stirlings, which protrude over the track, but he looks quickly away again and the woman does not look at all.

'Here we are, sir,' the sergeant says at last. The man says 'Thank you,' but the woman does not speak.

They have come to a long one-storied building, painted grey, with 'Squadron Headquarters' in white letters on the door. The sergeant opens the door for them and they go in, the man flapping and shaking the umbrella as he closes it down.

The office of the Wing Commander is at the end of a passage; the sergeant taps on the door, opens it and salutes. As the man and woman follow him, the man first, taking off his hat, the woman hangs a little behind, her face passive.

'Mr. and Mrs. Shepherd, sir,' the sergeant says.

'Oh, yes, good afternoon.' The sergeant, saluting, closes the door and goes.

'Good afternoon, sir,' the man says.

The woman does not speak.

'Won't you please sit down, madam?' the Wing Commander says. 'And you too, sir. Please sit down.'

He pushes forward two chairs, and slowly the man and the woman sit down, the man leaning his weight on the umbrella.

The office is small and there are no more chairs. The Wing Commander remains standing, his back resting against a table, beyond which, on the wall, the flight formations are ticketed up.

He is quite young, but his eyes, which are glassy and grey, seem old and focused distantly so that he seems to see far beyond the man and the woman and even far beyond the grey-green Stirlings lined up on the dark tarmac in the rain. He folds his arms across his chest and is glad at last when the man looks up at him and speaks.

'We had your letter, sir. But we felt we should like to come and see you, too.'

'I am glad you came.'

'I know you are busy, but we felt we must come. We felt you wouldn't mind.'

'Not at all. People often come.'

'There are just some things we would like to ask you.'

'I understand.'

The man moves his lips, ready to speak again, but the words do not come. For a moment his lips move like those of someone who stutters, soundlessly, quite helplessly. His hands grip hard on the handle of the umbrella, but still the words do not come and at last it is the Wing Commander who speaks.

'You want to know if everything possible was done to eliminate an accident?'

The man looked surprised that someone should know this, and can only nod his head.

'Everything possible was done.'

'Thank you, sir.'

'But there are things you can never foresee. The weather forecast may say, for example, no cloud over Germany, for perhaps sixteen hours, but you go over and you find a thick layer of cloud all the way, and you never see your target – and perhaps there is severe icing as you come home.'

'Was it like this when—'

'Something like it. You never know. You can't be certain.'

Suddenly, before anyone can speak again, the engines of a Stirling close by are revved up to a roar that seems to shake the walls of the room; and the woman looks up, startled, as if terrified that the 'plane will race forward and crash against the windows. The roar of airscrews rises furiously and then falls again, and the sudden rise and fall of sound seems to frighten her into speech.

'Why aren't you certain? Why can't you be certain? He should never have gone out! You must know that! You must know it! You must know that he should never have gone!'

'Please,' the man says.

'Day after day you are sending out young boys like this. Young boys who haven't begun to live. Young boys who don't know what life is. Day after day you send them out and they don't come back and you don't care! You don't care!'

She is crying bitterly now and the man puts his arm on her shoulder. She is wearing a fur and he draws it a fraction closer about her neck.

'You don't care, do you! You don't care! It doesn't matter to you. You don't care!'

'Mother,' the man says.

Arms folded, the Wing Commander looks at the floor, silently waiting for her to stop. She goes on for a minute or more longer, shouting and crying her words, violent and helpless, until at last she is exhausted and stops. Her fur slips off her shoulder and falls to the ground, and the man picks it up and holds it in his hands, helpless, too.

The Wing Commander walks over to the window and looks out. The airscrews of the Stirling are turning smoothly, shining like steel pin-wheels in the rain, and now, with the woman no longer shouting, the room seems very silent, and finally the Wing Commander walks back across the room and stands in front of the man and woman again.

'You came to ask me something,' he says.

'Take no notice, sir. Please. She is upset.'

'You want to know what happened? Isn't that it?'

'Yes, sir. It would help us a little, sir.'

The Wing Commander says very quietly: 'Perhaps I can tell you a little. He was always coming to me and asking to go out on operations. Most of them do that. But he used to come and beg to be allowed to go more than most. So more often than not it was a question of stopping him from going rather than making him go. It was a question of holding him back. You see?'

'Yes, sir.'

'And whenever I gave him a trip he was very happy. And the crew were happy. They liked going with him. They liked being together, with him, because they liked him so much and they trusted him. There were seven of them and they were all together.'

The woman is listening, slightly lifting her head.

'It isn't easy to tell you what happened on that trip. But we know that conditions got suddenly very bad and that there was bad cloud for a long way. And we know that they had navigational difficulties and that they got a long way off their course.

'Even that might not have mattered, but as they were coming back the outer port engine went. Then the radio transmitter went and the receiver. Everything went wrong. The wireless operator somehow got the transmitter and the receiver going again, but then they ran short of petrol. You see, everything was against him.'

'Yes, sir.'

'They came back the last hundred miles at about a thousand feet. But they trusted him completely, and he must have known they trusted him. A crew gets like that – flying together gives them this tremendous faith in each other.'

'Yes, sir.'

'They trusted him to get them home, and he got them home. Everything was against him. He feathered the outer starboard engine and then, in spite of everything, got them down on two engines. It was a very good show. A very wonderful show.'

The man is silent, but the woman lifts her head. She looks at the Wing Commander for a moment or two, immobile, very steady, and then says, quite distinctly, 'Please tell us the rest.'

'There is not much,' he says. 'It was a very wonderful flight, but they were out of luck. They were up against all the bad luck in the world. When they came to land they couldn't see the flarepath very well, but he got them down. And then, as if they hadn't had enough, they came down slightly off the runway and hit an obstruction. Even then they didn't crash badly. But it must have thrown him and he must have hit his head somewhere with great force, and that was the end.'

'Yes, sir. And the others?' the man says.

'They were all right. Even the second pilot. I wish you could have talked to them. It would have helped if you could have talked to them. They know that he brought them home. They know that they owe everything to him.'

'Yes, sir.'

The Wing Commander does not speak, and the man very slowly puts the fur over the woman's shoulders. It is like a signal for her to get up, and as she gets to her feet the man stands up too, straightening himself, no longer leaning on the umbrella.

'I haven't been able to tell you much,' the Wing Commander says. 'It's just the way it is.'

'It's everything,' the man says.

For a moment the woman still does not speak, but now she stands quite erect. Her eyes are quite clear, and her lips, when she does speak at last, are quite calm and firm.

'I know now that we all owe something to him,' she says. 'Good-bye.'

'Good-bye, madam.'

'Good-bye, sir,' the man says.

'You are all right for transport?'

'Yes, sir. We have a taxi.'

'Good. The sergeant will take you back.'

'Good-bye, sir. Thank you.'

'Good-bye,' the woman says.

'Good-bye.'

They go out of the office. The sergeant meets them at the outer door, and the man puts up the umbrella against the rain. They walk away along the wet perimeter, dwarfed once again by the grey-green noses of the Stirlings. They walk steadfastly, almost proudly, and the man holds the umbrella a little higher than before, and the woman, keeping up with him now, lifts her head.

And the Wing Commander, watching them from the window, momentarily holds his face in his hands.

THE SUN RISES TWICE

PERHAPS THE FINEST pilot I ever knew was Eddington-Green, whom we called E.G. He had no medals.

E.G. was small, a compact man, with cool, light, devilish, imperturbable eyes. His hands were surprisingly large for so small a man. On each hand the muscle between the thumb and forefinger, on the back of the hand, was very powerful. It stood out like a swelling.

He had made it hard and powerful by ju-jitsu, but he was afraid of practising the ju-jitsu any longer for fear of hurting, perhaps killing, someone. He looked a small man to kill anybody.

Pilots are often interested in nothing but popsies, kites, and beer. E.G. was interested in many things: so many that I never found out about them all. He raced motor-cars and collected stamps; he was interested in ships, had served in the Navy, and was a good radiographer. He had surprising tastes in advanced music; he was a good revolver shot and he was fond of flowers.

One of the few things he was not interested in, it seemed, was getting drunk. There were few parties for E.G. He did not stay up for those occasions, after ops., when air-crews relieve their feelings by doing trapeze acts over sofas.

After a long, hard trip he would come into the mess quite

quietly; drink a small light ale; warm his hands by the fire and talk for a few minutes; say that the trip was good or bad, in about as many words, and then go to bed.

It was almost a tradition that no one ever came home before him. No one flew a Stirling so fast and no one, except E.G. himself, knew why.

There was once an occasion when a force of Stirlings, owing to some sudden change of weather at base, was recalled from Northern Germany. All the kites, except E.G., were but seventy miles short of their target. E.G. was over the target. He was not long over the target, but he remained there long enough to do a circus act with a ring of searchlights, shooting them out one by one before turning for home. This shook even Intelligence. 'You've no business to have got so far,' they said.

There is no doubt, of course, that he had been there. He had been there simply because he said so. E.G. never shot a false line, or claimed a target unless he was sure.

The secret of his flying so fast was a trick, but it also had something artistic in it. It was one of those things he was never tired of working out for himself; and which seemed so simple when it was done. In the same way he used to watch the reactions of himself and other people to living and flying. He used to note how calm and clear and sure and icy he became in the periods when he did not drink at all. He used to note how shaky and sometimes how short-lived were those who did.

In E.G.'s squadron there was at one time a man named Tusser; a big crude ex-civil pilot, who hated Stirlings. Tusser, heavy and bullying, would be badly whistled six non-operational nights out of seven. E.G., who knew why Tusser was whistled and why he bullied and why he hated Stirlings, said, 'I give him six more trips.' Two trips later Tusser did not return.

I don't want to give the impression that E.G. was perfect; but that he was interested not only in flying but also in the things that flying does to men. I shall say nothing about the time he calmly formated with two Me. 109s, he himself flying solo, in an Anson trainer.

I liked to hear him describe the feelings and the sight of flight: the solo loneliness, the tracer coming up at you slow and orange until the last furious flashing moment, the moon over the miles and miles of cotton cloud, the flak so thick and many-coloured that it hung in the night air like paper streamers at a ball.

I liked to hear him talk of the time when he was coming home from a night trip to France. It was summer and he was flying at about eighteen thousand watching the sun rising over the sea. In the serene and beautiful air the sun floated upwards like an orange behind the rim of the yellow horizon. Below was a solitary ship, which the navigator reported was smoking badly.

E.G., always curious, put the aircraft into a turn, and, going back, went down to about ten thousand in order to look at her. From that height, in the clear summer morning air, he took the ship to be a merchantman of about nine thousand tons and he took her now to be smoking quite naturally, as if she were stoking up. So he turned the aircraft away, keeping the same height, and headed her again towards England.

And then, from that lower altitude, he saw an amazing thing. He saw the sun just trying to float upward over the horizon: rising for the second time on the same day.

If it had not been for a sense of great curiosity, a strong independent persistence, E.G. would never have seen this at all. It was as if he was living part of his life twice over. This quality of curiosity and independence, which made him test his reactions to drink and work out devices for flying faster and turn back to look at solitary ships that might be in trouble, made him the kind of pilot he was, and once, when he was flying Stirlings, almost finished him as a pilot altogether. His life would have been so much easier, so much smoother, and so much duller if he had kept to other people's rules instead of making his own.

The weather was not very good when he set out that afternoon to fly into Holland, to attack somewhere inland a target whose name I have forgotten.

It was late December and the weather had been intermittently dirty for several weeks. As E.G. crossed the coast somewhere beyond Scheveningen the weather suddenly closed down, dark and rainy, and he knew after a few minutes that the chances of seeing the target had gone. There was only one other aircraft with him, and after he had called it up they decided to turn back to sea. 'Keep to the coast,' E.G. said. 'We may see a little shipping.'

He lost sight of the other aircraft, but his own peculiar independent curiosity made him turn down towards the Hook of Holland instead of out to the open sea. In a couple of hours, if he had been sensible, he could have been eating lobster paste, Swiss roll, or smiling at the W.A.A.F. waitresses, fresh with their afternoon lipstick, in the mess. Instead, he turned the aircraft south-westward, just beyond sight of the coast, to look for shipping.

It was about ten minutes later that his navigator, a big husky Canadian, who was never really happy except when fighting, called out over the inter-comm. that he could see a tanker below. E.G. turned and saw her too; she seemed quite large; he thought perhaps about twelve thousand tons.

He saw, too, that she had two other ships with her, and they seemed very small beside her. They seemed so small, indeed, that he took them for tugs that had come out to meet her from the coast. It was a great mistake: as he found out later.

He turned away at once to make his first bombing run. The weather was clearer now. The cloud was higher, with breaks in it. There was no rain. He took his time and came in level and low, but not too low, dead over the tanker, and the navigator let go about a third of his bombs.

As he came down, the little escort ships, which he had thought were tugs, hit him with a surprising blaze of fire. He knew then what they were: not tugs, but escort flak ships, and they had holed his starboard wing.

From then he could have turned and gone safely home to lobster paste, Swiss roll, and the W.A.A.F.s in their cool blue uniforms pouring the tea. Instead, he drew away for a second bombing run. He came in level and low again. The flak was heavier than ever now and when he drew out again the aircraft, rocking badly, was full of smoke. Even then he could have gone home. Instead, he called the navigator.

'How many left, Mac?'

'Seven.'

'O.K.,' he said. 'This time.'

He drew away for the third time. He drew away much farther this time and came in much lower, so that the gunners could use their guns. He came in just over the mast of the tanker.

He saw the crew running across the deck. He saw them fall over each other, over the gear lying on the decks; and down the open hatches. He saw the tracer fire swinging up from the flak ships, like a series of violent orange balls thrown by a conjurer, first casual, then very fast, flying all about him as he dived.

He felt everything suddenly dissolve in a tremendous blast of fire. He felt that his ear-drums had been smashed. He could not see. 'This is it,' he thought. 'We've had it. This is it.'

He tried to pull the 'plane out of the dive that had taken them so low that it seemed they must clip off the mast of the ship, but for a few moments she would not come. She went soaring along, rocking violently, just above the dirty surface of the sea.

He strained hard to pull her out, and at last, slowly and heavily, she came out and began to climb. At that moment, too, his hearing came back. He heard a raging confusion of excited voices over the inter-comm. The whole crew seemed to be shouting wildly, and what they were shouting shook him for a moment worse than the flak, the explosion, and the dive had done.

'For God's sake. Fighters!'

He did not realize until that moment what had happened, that the tanker had been steaming steadily into port and that he had been following her in. He suddenly saw below him the flat, grey edge of coast; then the dark line of fighters coming up astern from the land. He had just time to see the black smoke of burning tanker ballooning up below him before he turned out to sea.

He realized at once that the 'plane would not manoeuvre. He was flying at about three hundred feet, perhaps less, above the sea. The afternoon was already darkening. Heavy cloud was driving in from the land. His speed was down to about a hundred and thirty, and he could neither increase it nor climb.

The 'plane was dead and heavy and soon the yelling in the inter-comm., which had temporarily ceased, began again. 'They're coming bloody close, E.G.,' the navigator said. 'Jeez, they're bloody close.'

The 'plane would still not manoeuvre and he still could not increase the speed, but at that last moment he induced her to climb. She climbed very slowly to six or seven hundred feet and as he made height he saw ahead of him a patch of dirty cloud. He went into it and when finally he came out of it, ten minutes later, the fighters were no longer to be seen.

He came home all the way, in half darkness and then in total darkness, through heavy rain, at what is sometimes jovially described as nought feet. He had only three engines and his speed was never more than a hundred and thirty. He could not see the flare-path well, and he landed too fast, lucky to land at all. It was a brave, exciting, shaky do.

'Did you prang the tanker?' Intelligence said.

'She was smoking.'

'But did you hit it?'

'We wouldn't claim it,' E.G. said. 'We're not sure.'

'Mac?'

'Jeez,' Mac said, 'we gave 'em hell. I don't claim no more than that. That's all I know.'

Intelligence, who is very charming, smiled.

'Are you bloody crazy?' he said, 'or don't you care?'

E.G., who is also charming, but who claims no hit he does not see, who never drinks because he remembers his crew, who flies faster than anyone else and makes his own rules and has no medals, smiled back in answer.

'A little of both,' he said.

They gave him no medals for that. But perhaps he is the sort of man who needs no medals.

The sun rises twice for him.

NO TROUBLE AT ALL

THE DAY WAS to be great in the history of the Station; it was just my luck that I didn't come back from leave until late afternoon. All day the sunlight had been a soft orange colour and the sky a clear wintry blue, without mist or cloud. There was no one in the mess ante-room except a few of the night-staff dozing before the fire, and no one I could talk to except the little W.A.A.F. who sits by the telephone.

So I asked her about the show. 'Do you know how many have gone?' I said.

'Ten, sir,' she said.

'Any back yet?'

'Seven were back a little while ago,' she said. 'They should all be back very soon.'

'When did they go? This morning?'

'Yes sir. About ten o'clock.' She was not young; but her face was pleasant and eager and, as at the moment, could become alight. 'They looked marvellous as they went, sir,' she said. 'You should have seen them, sir. Shining in the sun.'

'Who isn't back? You don't know?'

But she did know.

'K for Kitty and L for London aren't back,' she said. 'But I don't know the other.'

'It must be Brest again?' I said.

'Yes, sir,' she said. 'I think it's Brest.'

I didn't say anything, and she said, 'They are putting you in Room 20 this time, sir.'

'Thank you. I'll go up,' I said.

As I went upstairs and as I bathed and changed I made calculations. It was half-past three in the afternoon and the winter sun was already growing crimson above the blue edges of flat ploughed land beyond the Station buildings. I reckoned up how far it was to Brest. If you allowed half an hour over the target and a little trouble getting away, even the stragglers should be back by four. It seemed, too, as if fog might come down very suddenly; the sun was too red and the rim of the earth too blue. I realized that if they were not back soon they wouldn't be back at all. They always looked very beautiful in the sun, as the little W.A.A.F. said, but they looked still more beautiful on the ground. I didn't know who the pilot of L for London was; but I knew, and was remembering, that K for Kitty was my friend.

By the time I went downstairs again the lights were burning in the ante-room but the curtains were not drawn and the evening, sunless now, was a vivid electric blue beyond the windows. The little W.A.A.F. still sat by the telephone and as I went past she looked up and said:

'L for London is back, sir.'

I went into the ante-room. The fire was bright and the first crews, back from interrogation, were warming their hands. Their faces looked raw and cold. They still wore sweaters and flying boots and their eyes were glassy.

'Hullo,' they said. 'You're back. Good leave?' They spoke as if it was I, not they, who had been three hundred miles away.

'Hullo, Max,' I said. 'Hullo, Ed. Hullo, J.B.'

I had been away for five days. For a minute I felt remote; I couldn't touch them.

I was glad when someone else came in.

'Hullo. Good trip?'

'Quite a picnic.'

'Good. See anything?'

'Everything.'

'Good show, good show. Prang them?'

'Think so. Fires burning when we got there.'

'Good show.'

I looked at their faces. They were tired and hollow. In their eyes neither relief nor exhilaration had begun to filter through the glassiness of long strain. They talked laconically, reluctantly, as if their lips were frozen.

'Many fighters?'

'Hordes.'

'Any trouble?'

'The whole bloody crew was yelling fighters. Came up from everywhere.'

'Any Spits?'

'Plenty. Had five Me.'s on my tail. Then suddenly wham! Three Spits came up from nowhere. Never saw anything like those Me.'s going home for tea.'

'Good show. Good show.'

The evening was darkening rapidly and the mess-steward came in to draw the curtains. I remembered K for Kitty and suddenly I went out of the ante-room and stood for a moment in the blue damp twilight, listening and looking at the sky. The first few evening stars were shining and I could feel that later the night would be frosty. But there was no sound of a plane.

I went back into the ante-room at last and for a moment, in the bright and now crowded room, I could not believe my eyes. Rubbing his cold hands together, his eyes remote and chilled, his sweater hanging loose below his battle-dress, the pilot of K for Kitty was standing by the fireplace. There was a cross of flesh-pink plastic bandage on his forehead and I knew that something had happened.

'Hullo,' I said.

'Hullo,' he said. 'You're back.'

For a minute I didn't say anything else. I wanted to shake his hand and tell him I was glad he was back. I knew that if he had been in a train-wreck or a car crash I should have shaken his hand and told him I was glad. Now somebody had shot him up and all I said was:

'When did you get in?'

'About an hour ago.'

'Everything O.K.?'

'Wrapped her up.'

'Well,' I said. 'Just like that?'

'Just like that,' he said.

I looked at his eyes. They were bleared and wet and excited. He had made a crash landing; he was safe; he was almost the best pilot in the outfit.

'Anyone see me come in?' he said.

'Saw you from Control,' someone said.

'How did it look?'

'Perfect until the bloody airscrew fell off.'

Everyone laughed: as if airscrews falling off were a great joke. Nobody said anything about anybody being lucky to be back, but only:

'Have an argument?'

'Flak blew bloody great bit out of the wing. The inter-comm. went and then both turrets.'

'Many fighters?'

'Ten at a time.'

'Get one?'

'One certain. Just dissolved. One probable.'

'Good show. What about the ships?'

'I think we pranged them.'

'Good show,' we said. 'Good show.'

We went on talking for a little longer about the trip: beautiful weather, sea very blue, landscape very green in the sun. And then he came back to the old subject.

'How did I land? What did it look like?'

'Beautiful.'

'I couldn't get the tail down. Both tyres were punctured.'

'Perfect all the same.'

He looked quite happy. It was his point of pride, the good landing; all he cared about now. With turrets gone, fuselage like a colander, wings holed, and one airscrew fallen off, he had nevertheless brought her down. And though we all knew it must have been hell no one said a word.

Presently his second dicky came into the ante-room. He was very young, about nineteen, with a smooth aristocratic face and smooth aristocratic hair. He looked too young to be part of a war and he was very excited.

'Went through my sleeve.'

He held up a cannon shell. Then he held up his arm. There was a neat tear in the sleeve of his battle-dress. He was very proud.

Across the knuckles of his right hand there was a thread line of dried blood, neat, fine, barely visible. He wetted his other forefinger and rubbed across it, as if to be sure it wouldn't wash away.

'Came in on the starboard side and out the other.'

'Good show,' said somebody quite automatically. 'Good show.'

'Anybody hurt?' I asked.

'Engineer.'

'Very bad?'

'Very bad. I bandaged him and gave him a shot coming home.'

As he went on talking I looked down at his knees. There were dark patches on them, where blood had soaked through his flying-suit. But all that anyone said was:

'Think you pranged them?'

'Oh! sure enough. They've had it this time.'

'Good show,' we said. 'Good show.'

Now and then, as we talked, the little W.A.A.F. would come in from the telephone to tell someone he was wanted. With her quiet voice she would break for a moment the rhythm of excitement that was now rising through outbursts of laughter to exhilaration. She would hear for a second or two a snatch of the now boisterous but still laconic jargon of flight, 'Think we may have pranged in, old boy. Good show. Piece of cake. No trouble at all,' but there would be no sign on her calm and rather ordinary face that it conveyed anything to her at all. Nor did the crews, excited by the afternoon, the warmth and the relief of return, take any notice of her. She was an automaton, negative, outside of them, coming and going and doing her duty.

Outside of them, too, I listened and gathered together and finally pieced together the picture of the raid; and then soon afterwards the first real pictures of operations were brought in for the Wing Commander to see, and for a moment there was a flare of excitement. We could see the bomb-bursts across the battleships and the quays and then smoke over the area of town and docks. 'You think we pranged them, sir?' we said.

'Pranged them? Like hell we did.'

'Good show. Bloody good show.'

'Slap across the Gluckstein.'

'No doubt this time?'

'No doubt.'

'Good show,' we said. 'Good show.'

At last, when the photographs had been taken away again, I went out of the ante-room into the hall. As I walked across it the little W.A.A.F., sitting by the telephone, looked up at me.

'A wonderful show, sir,' she said.

I paused and looked at her in astonishment. I wondered for a moment how she could possibly know. There had been no time for her to hear the stories of the crews; she had not seen the photographs; she did not know that K for Kitty had been wrapped up and that it must have been hell to land on two dud tyres and with a broken airscrew; she did not know that the ships had been hit or that over Brest, on that bright calm afternoon, it had been partly magnificent and partly hell.

'How did you know?' I said.

She smiled a little and lifted her face and looked through the glass door of the ante-room.

'You can tell by their faces, sir,' she said.

I turned and looked too. In the morning we should read about it in the papers; we should hear the flat bulletins; we should see the pictures. But now we were looking at something that could be read nowhere except in their eyes and expressed in no language but their own.

'Pretty good show,' I said.

'Yes, sir,' she said. 'No trouble at all.'

A PERSONAL WAR

HE IS A little fellow with an oval head that is quite bald except for a few feathery wisps of grey hair. He has a small tobacco-gold moustache, and sharp blue eyes and a way of bowing slightly when he speaks to you: as if he were nothing but the receptionist of a hotel, or a cashier at a bank, or a traveller in toys.

It is not until you look at his hands that you realize that they are not the hands of a man who books rooms for guests or counts money or winds up the keys of little engines. They are very short and thick and powerful hands and the fingertips protrude unusually far beyond the small tight nails. Then after you have looked at his hands, which are so small yet so muscular and aggressive, you look back at his face, and you see then that the little stiff moustache and the sharp blue eyes and even the bald grey head are aggressive too, and that even the short and charming bow has another meaning. After talking to him for a little while you realize what this meaning is. He is a traveller in a Stirling, and his toys are guns.

We sit talking for a long time before he tells me this. It is winter and at the moment there are no operations. Still grey mists hang far over the flat land, and pools of yellow mud cover the track along which the bombers are lined up. It has been raining for a long time and there is no wind to drive the mist away.

Suddenly, for no reason, he talks of America.

'You have been there?' I say.

'For a long time,' he says. 'I was born here, but mostly I lived there.'

'Where?'

'In Texas mostly.'

'Which is why they call you Tex?'

'Which is why they call me Tex,' he says, with a smile.

'And how,' I say, 'do you feel about America?'

'America or Americans?'

'Americans.'

'Which Americans?' he says.

We both laugh. I look out of the window and watch for a moment the rain dripping down through the mist on the huge iron-coloured wings of the Stirlings, and when I look back at him again I see that he has stopped laughing and is serious again.

'You think they don't understand?' I say.

'Not only that.'

'What else?'

'It's not only time they understand,' he says, 'it's time they got angry. It's time they got good and angry too.'

'Like you?'

'A bit more like me,' he says.

He smiles and we sit without talking for a little while and I watch his hands. He has a way of crooking the fingers of his right hand into the fingers of the left, and then pulling them, as if they were triggers. Finally I ask him if he will have a drink and with a charming smile but without uncrooking his hands he says: 'Possibly. Thank you. Possibly I will. It is very kind of you. Thank you.'

'What will it be?'

'Thank you,' he says. 'A beer.'

When the beer comes I ask him what it is like up there, in the rear-turret, on ops. – if he gets bored or tired or very cold, and he says, 'No. Only just angry. Very good and angry all the time.' I listen and soon he goes on to tell me about the flak: how it seems to come up slowly, very slowly, as if it will never climb into the darkness.

'Very bad too?'

'Not at all polite,' he says.

'And in Texas?' I say. 'What were you doing there?'

'Sheriff.'

'Gun and all?'

'Why sure,' he says. 'Gun and all. Notches and all.'

So he goes on to tell me about the life in Texas, the life of a boy's dream: the gun and the notches, the sheriff and the posse, the remote, enormous country. As he talks I try to see the life as something real, but it unfolds itself to me only like a series of glimpses into a dusky unreality. I cannot believe in the gun, the little sheriff's office in the little town, the dusty plains, the posse, and the notches whittled on the gun-stock. I cannot believe in the life of his America any more than he can understand, now, the minds of so many who go on living it.

So we talk about flying again. He has not flown for a week and as I look at him I see that the small blue eyes are sharp and fretful with impatience as much as with anger. 'My God, if I don't soon fly,' he says, 'I'll be swinging on the bloody chandelier.'

He finishes the beer. 'You will have another? Please. This time on me?'

I thank him and when the beer comes he talks a little more. There is a medal ribbon on his chest. It seems more real than the notches in the gun but I do not ask about it. Instead he tells me about a time when they stooged above the

51

Scharnhorst at Brest. It was the day they scored a hit, and he talks for a time about this, casually, without anger, as if it were an afternoon picnic. It is as though battleships were impersonal things and I know suddenly that what he likes is the personal feeling about it all: the feeling of cold isolation in the rear-turret, the sight of the flak climbing up in the darkness in slow coloured curls, the feeling of his own thick powerful hands on the guns.

I know that this is what he likes, but I still do not understand why he likes it. I do not understand why he likes it more than the life of a sheriff in a little Texas town, with his posse and his gun and the notches on the gun, as if he were a hero in a film. I do not understand why he has left that life, to fly in a country that is only half his own. I do not understand why he does not remain, like so many others, isolated, apart, away from it all.

And finally I ask him. 'You really like it up there, don't you?' I say.

'Like it?'

'Yes.'

For a moment he does not speak. Then he looks at me with a fierce little smile, his fingers tightly crooked into each other, his eyes screwed up, hard and intense.

'Like it?' he says. There is nothing of the receptionist or the bank cashier or the traveller in toys about him now. He is far removed even from the little sheriff in the little Texas town. His eyes are furious and the smile in his face is quite deadly. He is caught up by a raw hatred of someone or something that is almost sublime and he no longer leaves me in any doubt as to who it is.

'Like it? I was just born with a natural hatred of these swabs. I was born with it and all my life I've been living to work it off. Like it?' he says, 'it's a personal argument with me. It's a personal war.'

Now I understand, and suddenly I feel quite small and there is nothing I can say.

I can only look out of the windows at the huge dark Stirlings shining dully on the perimeter in the rain, and hope that soon there will be a wind that will drive the mist away.

K FOR KITTY

HARRISON WAS ONE of those lean, brown, old-eyed Australians who seem to accept England with a tolerance that Canadians never know. If there were things about England that needed changing or setting right Harrison rarely talked about them. If there were better pilots I rarely met them. Harrison was quiet, modest, friendly, and as tough as hell.

It was not Harrison, but someone else, who first talked to me of the idea that 'planes and ships have the same delicate and temperamental ways. Just as you find no two ships alike, so you find no two 'planes alike; just as you find ships that are heavy, graceless, unalive, so you find 'planes that are dull and wooden in the air. In the same way that seamen come to know, trust, and finally get fond of a ship, knowing that she is a living thing and will never fail them, so pilots come to know and trust and get fond of a 'plane, knowing she will bring them home. In every squadron there is, I suppose, a 'plane that everybody hates. Then one day somebody quietly wraps it up in a distant corner of the 'drome and everybody is relieved and glad. But in every squadron there is a 'plane that everyone likes that is something more than a pattern of steel and wood and instruments and mechanism, that is a living, graceful, fortunate, and ultimately triumphant thing, and this was the sort of 'plane that Harrison had.

Harrison's 'plane was a big four-engined Stirling called K for Kitty. The kite, like Harrison, was no stranger to the shaky do. On a trip to Brest the bomb doors froze up and would not release. This was bad enough. But the starboard outer also failed on the journey home; so that Harrison was obliged to land on three engines, with a full bomb load, in darkness: the sort of heroism for which, at the moment, we have struck no special gong. On other trips other things happened. Something happened to the flaps; the undercarriage jammed; the radio went u.s. – it does not matter. For the heroism of overcoming such minor misfortunes there are no gongs either.

After such trips Harrison naturally trusted and grew fond of K for Kitty. Not that I think he ever said so. He would call the kite a good kite or perhaps, if he were a little happy, a wizard kite. These events in K for Kitty bore, after all, only a very slight relation to suicide. It was not until the big Brest trip that anything really serious happened to the 'plane.

I am not sure if this raid, made on a clear blue winter afternoon when the sunlight was light orange-coloured and the horizon peaceful with light haze, was the biggest ever made on Brest. But that night many bottles were opened and many songs sung, and I conclude from that, at least, that it was very big. And among the many 'planes that went Harrison was in K for Kitty.

Nor am I sure if they tried to blow Harrison to small pieces before he bombed, or after. Possibly both. Finally a force of Messerschmitts attacked him, in a rapid succession of ten, and put out of action every turret he had. Tracer tore at all angles through the nose and body of the 'plane. It shaved the skin off the knuckles of Harrison and his second dicky. It smashed the inter-comm. and mortally wounded the engineer. Blood flowed over the floor of the 'plane, mingling stickily with oil.

It was hard to stand up and the gunners could not fire and there were no warning voices in the inter-comm.

Many other things had happened that Harrison did not then know about, but was to know about later. He was glad enough to see Spitfires coming up as escort, and the Messerschmitts diving home to tea. He was glad to be out of it, and setting course for home again. He was quite glad that K for Kitty was his 'plane.

At home, in the bright calm golden air of the late winter afternoon, Harrison brought her down gently and beautifully, making a perfect landing. He even succeeded in holding for some distance to the runway. And then everything that had not already happened began to happen at once. It was as if the kite had blown home held together only by strips of sticky plaster and string; as if she were a toy 'plane, put together by children, that could not withstand the vibration of contact with earth.

She began to fall to pieces suddenly, terrifyingly, and almost systematically. The starboard outer airscrew fell off, and then the starboard inner engine fell out completely. Then the complete starboard wing fell off, and then both the fallen wing and the fallen engine caught fire. Just before she came to rest the port wing was flung high into the air like the arm of someone drowning, and remained there, high and stiff and awkward and dead.

I do not know how Harrison and the rest of the crew got out of the 'plane, slipping and skidding in the oily blood and lifting the wounded engineer, then skidding and falling down in the blood again, the 'plane burning all the time, the main door jammed and only the forward hatch available for lifting to safety the heavy wounded man. It seemed at any moment that the 'plane might blow up. But somehow Harrison and the crew and the wounded man got out and the 'plane did not blow up.

She was still there, in that lopsided, high-flung position, flat-tyred, partially burnt, when I went across the field next morning. Harrison was there too, looking at her. He was pacing up and down. The burnt, ash-covered wreckage of the 'plane lay scattered in an almost straight line across the grass. Beyond the last grey scraps of wreckage the tyre marks of the 'plane made brown parallel lines in the muddy grass as far as the runway. Harrison walked up the tracks made by the flattened tyres, stooped down to look at them and then walked back, stooping down again. Finally he came back to the 'plane.

We stood there for a long time together, looking at the 'plane. We picked up scraps of wreckage and dropped them again in the grass. We looked at the flattened tyres and the broken undercarriage and the splintered turret. We examined the ugly rising lines of tracer holes, neat and straight as the crotchets of a raising scale punched everywhere across the flat face of the fuselage. We stood under the high, up-flung wing, smashed by flak, that looked more than ever like a stiff dead arm. We looked at everything in amazement and unbelief and then looked again.

Long after I left, Harrison was still standing by the 'plane. And once, as I walked across the field, I turned and looked back.

He was still standing there in the same attitude, looking at K for Kitty. I could not see his face, but it seemed as if he were looking at something rather distantly. It seemed even possible that he was looking at something he could not see.

It was like the attitude of a seaman who looks across empty water, for the last time, and sees his ship no longer there.

THE GREATEST PEOPLE
IN THE WORLD

HE WAS VERY young, and because he was also very fair, he sometimes looked too young to have any part in the war at all; and more than anything else, as always, he wanted to fly.

It was his fairness that made him look so very much like one of the aristocracy, or at least very upper middle class, and I was very surprised to find that his people were labourers from a village in Somerset. His father was a hedger and ditcher with a fancy for leaving little tufts of hawthorn unclipped above the line of hedge. These tufts would grow into little ornamental balls, and later were clipped, gradually, summer by summer, into the shapes of birds. His father hoped, Lawson would explain to me, that bullfinches would use them for nesting-places. I never met either his father or his mother, but I gathered that they must have been at least forty when he was born. I gathered too that his mother cleaned at the local rectory and that she worked in the fields, harvesting and hay-making and pea-picking and cabbage-planting, whenever she had the chance or the time.

It was not only that Lawson wanted to fly. He had never wanted to do anything else but fly. It was the only life he had had time to know. There must have been thousands of young men like him, all reading the technicalities of the job in flight magazines, all passionately studying new designs, all longing for a flip, all flying Spitfires in imagination. But there were certain circumstances which made the case of Lawson different.

The chief of these circumstances, and the one which was in fact never altered, was that his parents were poor. When Lawson heard other people with incomes of five or six hundred or more a year talking of having no money he thought of his parents. His father knocked up a regular wage of two pounds a week. In summer he managed to increase this by ten or twelve shillings by gardening in the evenings and his mother put in a weekly average of about sixteen hours at sixpence an hour at the rectory. As a boy, Lawson went harvesting and haymaking for about sixpence a day and doing odd jobs on Saturdays in the rectory kitchen. And somehow, out of this, they bought him an education.

I don't know who was at the back of this idea of education. It may have been the rector. Most likely it was the rector and the mother. Lawson's father, I gathered, was a solid, unimaginative man who was rather content to let things remain as they were. He worked hard for three hundred and sixty-two days of the year – he tended his own garden on Sundays – and then got roaring tight on Christmas Eve, Flower Show Saturday, and the local Easter Monday races. It obviously wasn't he who had the idea of education, yet once the idea had been conceived he was behind it wholly and with all the solidity of his nature. For two years he and his mother saved up every extra penny they earned; every pea picked, every potato picked up, every forkful of hay turned over was something extra to the account. The house where they lived was old and damp, with unplastered walls and a brick floor and cracks in the window-frames that were stuffed with paper. The only light they had was a little oil lamp which they carried from room to room if they wanted a light in another place. They bought half a hundredweight of coal each week and on Friday afternoons the mother wetted the last shovelful of coal and banked up the fire so that it would last till evening.

When Lawson was fourteen they were able to send him to the local grammar school. Or at least they were going to send him. Everything was arranged for him to start in September when one of those little accidents happened that often greatly affect the course of people's lives. Lawson fell off a bridge and broke his left arm. By the time it was better the vacancies in the first school were filled and he was sent instead to a school about fifteen miles away. He travelled there every day by train.

It was at this school that he heard the remark that was to affect, and crystallize, his whole life. The third term he was there, within a week or so of his fifteenth birthday, he heard a lecture in the school hall on the work of the R.A.F. When the lecture began, he told me, he really wasn't very interested. When he came out he could not get out of his mind something the lecturer had said about those who fly. 'I often think', the lecturer said, 'that they are the greatest people in the world.'

When I knew Lawson the war was two years old. He had graduated rather uneventfully in the usual way, up through Moths and Ansons and so to light bombers, until now he was captain of a Stirling. There was even then a kind of premature immobility about him, especially about his eyes, so that the pupils sometimes looked seared, cauterized, burnt out. His first trouble was to have been made a bomber pilot at all. He had been through the usual Spitfire complex; all roaring glory and victory rolls. The thought of long flights of endurance, at night, with nothing to be seen except the flak coming up at you in slow sinister curls, the earth in the light of a flare, and then the flare-path at base if you were lucky and the fog hadn't come down, shook him quite a lot. It may have been this that accounted for what happened afterwards.

He stayed at school until he was eighteen, and had virtually walked straight out of school into the Air Force. What struck me most was that there was no disruption, no disloyalty, between himself and his parents. There might well have been. Their life, simple, bound to earth, lighted by that cheap paraffin lamp which they carried from room to room, compressed into the simple measure of hard work, saving, and devotion, was like the life of another age compared with the life they had chosen for him. I don't know what education exactly meant to them; I don't know what ambitions they had for him. But neither could have been connected with his flying a bomber. Yet they never uttered the smallest reproach or protest to what must have been rather a terrifying prospect to them. They might have thought that it would be better for him to be ploughing his own good Somerset clay. They probably did. But if they did they didn't once say so. They simply knew he wanted to fly and they let him fly because it was the thing that was nearest his heart.

His own part was just as straightforward and steadfast. As I became acquainted with it I didn't wonder at all that he had been made a bomber pilot. The qualities for it were all there in his behaviour towards these two simple, self-sacrificial people. They had sent him to a pretty expensive school – to them it must have been fabulous – and he might easily have turned his back on them. A touch of swollen head and he might easily have decided that he was too good for that shabby little cottage, with the unplastered walls, the windows stuffed with paper, and the one cheap paraffin lamp carried from room to room. But I don't suppose he ever dreamed of it. He not only remained loyal to them but loyal in a positive way. He sent home to them a third of his pay every month: which for a Pilot Officer meant practically the same sacrifice as they had made for him.

He couldn't in fact have been more steadfast and careful. Perhaps he was too steadfast and, if it's possible as the captain of a crew of seven in a very expensive piece of aircraft, too careful. Yet nothing went right for him. Before his first big trip with a Stirling he felt the same dry mental tension, and the same sour wet slackness of the stomach, that you feel before a race. It was a sort of cold excitement. He felt it get worse as he taxied the aircraft across the field. It was winter and there was a kind of smokiness in the falling twilight over the few distant trees, and the hangars, looming up with their red lights burning, looked enormous. The runway seemed foreshortened and it looked practically impossible not to prang something on take-off. He was certain it would be all right once he was up, but it was the idea of lugging thirty-two tons of aircraft off the wet runway, that was soft in places, and in half-light, which worried him.

He was worked up to a very high state of tension, with the kite actually on the runway, when Control informed him that the whole show would be scrubbed. His crew swore and mouthed at everybody and everything all the way back to dispersal. He felt too empty to say anything. He felt as if his stomach had dropped out and that he might be going to pieces. The awful anti-climax of the thing was too much.

That night he didn't sleep very well. He fell asleep and then woke up. His blankets had slipped and he was very cold and he did not know what time it was. He could hear his watch ticking very loudly. Someone had left a light on in the passage outside and it shone through the fan-light of the bedroom door. He lay for hours watching it, sleepless, cold, his mind full of the impression of the wet runway, the hangars looming up in the twilight, the idea that he was about to prang something on take-off.

Then he fell asleep and dreamed that he really did prang

something. He was taking-off and his port wing hit the control tower, which had wide, deep, circular windows. Through these windows he could see Brand, the control officer, and a little Flying Officer named Danvers, and the two orderlies, one wearing earphones. The two officers were drinking tea and his wing knocked the cups out of their hands. The tea shot up in a brown wave that broke on Brand's tunic, and he saw vividly the look of helpless and terrified indignation on Brand's face a second before he was hit and died.

It was fantastic, but very real also, and he woke in a terrible sweat of fear, scared solely by the happenings of the dream. He was relieved to find it a waking dream; that it was already daylight beyond the drawn curtains. It was in fact already late and he got up hurriedly and went down to breakfast without shaving. After breakfast he went straight over to the hangars and hoped there would be flying that day. But the weather was worse: grey fenland distances, gathering ground mist, spits of cold rain. The Wing Commander usually got the crews running round the perimeter track for training, but that morning the weather was too bad, there was no running and by eleven o'clock the crews were fretting for an afternoon stand-down. Lawson went over to his aircraft, but everything was nicely fixed there and his stooges were sheltering under the wings, out of the rain, smoking. As he walked back in the rain to Control and went up the concrete stairs to the room where, in his dream, he had crashed through the wide windows and had killed Brand and Danvers, he saw at once that Brand and Danvers were not on duty, and by this fact, the fact that Brand and Danvers had been on duty at the time of the dream, he felt the reality of the dream grow brighter instead of fade.

After he had had the orderly bring him a cup of tea he

drank it quickly and then went out alone. The trouble was perhaps that he was at that time a stranger in the station. There was no one – and it must have been better if there had been someone – to whom he could say, joking: 'Had a hell of a queer dream last night. Dreamt I pranged the control tower. Brand was stooging around as usual and got it in the neck. He looked pretty damned funny when I knocked the tea out of his hands.' But he knew no one very well, and could say nothing about the dream. It was like a complex personal problem. Once you had explained it to someone else it was no longer personal; it ceased to be complex and finally it ceased to be a problem at all.

Unfortunately he could not do this, and unfortunately there was a recurrence of the dream that night. It was the same dream precisely, with one important exception. It was now not Brand and Danvers who were killed, but two men named Porter and Evans, the duty officers for that night. The painful brightness of the dream was identical; he could see the brown tea streaming as it splashed on Porter's jacket and he could see on his face, as on Brand's face, the indignant, ridiculous terror.

The next morning the weather was much better, and by noon it was certain there would be ops. that night. At briefing he felt much as if he had a hangover. He concentrated hard on the met. talk, but his head ached and the green and pink and mauve contour lines of the map troubled his eyes. The target was Hamburg, a fairly long hard trip, and his own take-off was at 18.00 hours. By the time he reached his aircraft the light was no longer good, but there was no mist and only thin cloud in a wasting blue sky. For some reason he now felt better: clearer-headed, quite confident. His stomach was dry and tight and the period of distrust in himself was practically over.

Then something else happened. His outer port engine

would not start. As he sat there in the aircraft, struggling to get things going, his crew on edge, his engineer bewildered and furious by this inexplicable behaviour of an engine that had been tested only that morning, he felt his confidence breaking down again. The light was dying rapidly on the fringes of the field and he knew what must happen any moment now. 'It's just one of these bloody damn things,' the engineer said over and over again. 'Just one of these damn bloody aggravating bastard things.' Some minutes later Lawson, not listening much now to the engineer, heard what he expected to hear from Control. The trip was off; the margin of time was past. 'Is it understood?' said Control in the voice of an ironical automatic parrot. 'Is it understood?'

After this second disappointment he went through the same nervous agony of not sleeping. Because the breaking of tension at a vital moment was the cause in both cases you might have said he was trying too hard. But the third occasion seemed to have nothing to do with this. He was again on operations, and again it was evening, with the fringes of the drome blue-grey with winter mist, the runway pooled with water, the red lights like beacons on the black mountains of the hangars. This time he actually got up off the runway. He had actually got over the sickening horror that for the third time running some damnable triviality would stop him from getting the kite airborne. But soon that was past, and he was following the others. The sun had already set, leaving huge cloud-broken lakes of pale green and yellow light for miles above the sunset point, and towards these immense spaces of rapidly fading light he watched the black wings of the Stirlings fading into the distance until at last it was too dark and the lakes of light and the 'planes were no longer there to see. Then for the first time for weeks he felt good: strained but calm, sure of himself, settled.

I suppose they had been flying about an hour when the icing began. They were over the sea when the kite began to make sickening and heavy plunges in the darkness: movements to which there was only one answer. Lawson felt suddenly up against all the old trouble again: the inexplicable bad luck, the frustration, the disastrous break of tension. He felt himself lose heart. His guts became wet and cold and sour and then seemed to drop out of him. His only piece of luck was that he had not flown far, and when he had safely jettisoned his bombs and turned the kite for home he bitterly told himself that it was the only piece of luck he had ever had as a pilot or was ever likely to have. But even that was not all. As he came in to land it was as if there were some evil and persistent Jonah in the kite with him: somebody for whom the simplest moments were inexplicably turned into pieces of hellish and ironical misfortune. Lawson landed perfectly in the darkness, but the runway was wet and greasy after rain. He put on the brakes, but nothing happened. The kite drove fast down the runway and then skidded into a ground loop that brought it to a standstill on the grass, the undercarriage smashed. To Lawson it was like the end of everything.

He expected to be grounded any moment after that. His despair was sour and keen and personal; he could tell no one about it. For about a week he did not sleep much. He did not dream either. He re-created the few moments of ill-luck until they were moments of positive and monstrous failure. And as if this were not enough he created new moments, sharp and terrible seconds of stalling, ground-looping, crash-landing, overshooting the drome. He imagined himself coming in too slow, another time too fast. It never mattered much. He was going to prang control tower in any case, killing the occupants there as they drank their last over-sweetened steaming tea.

Then by accident he discovered it possible to get some sleep. He began to sleep with the light on. The Station at that time was not very crowded; later two or even three people slept in a room. But now no one could see him giving way – not that he was ever the only one – to the fear of sleeping in the dark. In this way he slept quite well for about a week; it was fairly peaceful; he was not cold; he did not have the recurrent dream. And above all, they did not ground him.

I don't know if they were ever thinking of it; but it never in fact became necessary. Another thing happened: this time not just ill-luck, frustration, a mistake, a private illusion about something, but a simple and terrible fact. It was a telegram from the Rectory of his village in Somerset. His parents had been killed in a raid.

After that telegram he got compassionate leave and went home. The next morning he stood in the garden of the house, staring at the bony, burnt roof timbers, the red-grey dust and rubble, the bare scorched blue wall-paper, of the two rooms where the cheap little paraffin lamp had once been carried to and fro. It was winter time. Red dust lay on the frozen leaves of the brussels sprouts; the hawthorn twigs, fancifully clipped by his father above the line of hedge, were almost the only things about the place that remained untouched and as before. He did not stay very long; but while he stayed there he thought he saw his mother working in the fields, skirt pinned behind her, and his father with the hedge-hook in his hand and the black twigs flying in the air. He saw for a moment their lives with the simple clearness of grief, the lives remote from his own, so utterly simple and so utterly remote, yet bound to him elementally.

When he went back to the station three days later, he had forgotten about the dreams, the illusions, and all the rest of it; or at least it was as if he had forgotten. All the reality of the bad moments, if it had been reality, was now obscured by the simple reality of the dusty and fire-blackened little house.

All that he had to do now seemed also quite simple and clear; terribly simple and terribly clear. If he ever had been afraid, there was no longer any sign of it as he took off for a daylight raid over Northern Germany two days later. It was a cold, clear winter afternoon; there was just enough power in the sunlight to reveal the colours of the fields. He used to say it was one of those trips where you felt the aircraft had been shot from a gun. You got away clean and smooth and easy; there was no hitch. Instinctively, from the first, you knew it was a piece of cake. You went over and did the job and no matter what came up at you you knew that, ultimately, it would be all right. That afternoon flak tore a strip off his flaps and for about half an hour his crew did nothing but yell gloriously through the inter-comm. that fighters were coming up from everywhere. Cannon fire hit his middle turret and put it out of action and sprayed the fuselage from end to end with raw ugly little holes. Inland over Germany he lost a lot of height chasing and finally shooting down an Me. 109, and he discovered he could not regain his height as he came back over the coast and sea. But even that did not trouble him then. Everything was clear at last. His whole life was clear.

He came over the English coast and then the English fields, at about two or three hundred feet. The sun was still shining, but sometimes there were clouds and then it was light in patches on the fields below and dark in the upper air. He roared over fields and woods and roads and over the little dusty blue towns and over remote farms where he could even see the hens feeding and scuttling in the dark winter grass.

He came so low once that for a second or so he saw people in the fields. For an instant he saw a man and woman working. They raised flat, astonished faces to look at the great 'plane overhead. The woman perhaps was picking sticks and he thought he saw the man lean for a moment on a fork. They might have been old or young, he could not tell; they lifted their heads and in a second were cut off by the speed of the 'plane. But in this second, as he saw them transfixed on the earth below him and before the speed of the 'plane cut them off for ever, he remembered his own people. He remembered them as they lived, simple and sacrificing, living only for him, and he saw them alive again in the arrested figures of the two people in the field below: as if they were the same people, the same simple people, the same humble, faithful, eternal people, giving always and giving everything: the greatest people in the world.

IT'S NEVER IN THE PAPERS

EVERY MORNING WHEN I came downstairs I sat in the mess and looked at the papers. 'Last night our bombers,' I would read. 'Yesterday evening at dusk a strong formation.' But what I really looked for was never there.

I used to consider the case of Dibden. Dibden was twenty-five. He was a pilot with thirty-three operational trips and a D.F.C. to his name. He flew Stirlings and looked more than anything else like a dark, very handsome little Eskimo. You felt that it was a pure accident that he was flying a bomber instead of doing a roll in a kayak or having a snooze in an igloo.

Dibden was a good type, and a very good pilot indeed. But there were some who would not fly with him. Navigators, changed from their own crew, would suddenly develop violent toothache or trouble with their ears. Dibden was rather proud of the way he could land a Stirling in fair imitation of a golf-ball.

Once, on circuit and bumps, Dibden began to come in for landing with his air-speed down to ninety. He pulled her off again and did a sickly turn over the telegraph posts on the railway line and came back to land on the established golf-ball principle, hastily. 'It was quite a moment,' Dibden said.

There was nothing about that in the papers. Nor, of course,

was there anything about the way he had all his operational hours carefully added up. His thirty-three trips amounted to a hundred and fifty hours.

Very soon, with another fifty hours, Dibden would be a veteran; an old man of twenty-five who had watched others do their three and five and perhaps fifteen trips and not return. Dibden always returned; like a ball thrown at a wall he came back, and the harder you threw him the faster he returned.

Once or twice a week, when not on ops., Dibden got a little whistled, but the papers, of course, did not mention this either. You came into the mess late at night, tired, perhaps, after a spell of duty, to find Dibden bouncing from chair to chair, table to piano, like a smiling cherubic little Eskimo chasing an invisible bear.

At intervals he stopped being the Eskimo and became the bear, rushing up to other people, especially newcomers, to embrace them. 'Bad type, bad type!' he would say. 'Seize him, knock him down. Bad type!' We were all bad types when Dibden was whistled, but the papers, of course, did not mention this either. We are very good types really.

After these adventures others came down to breakfast with faces looking the colour of the sheepskin on their flying-boots; they looked at the mess of kidneys and bacon and said, 'My God, I've had it,' and crawled away.

But not Dibden. He bounced in very late, more cherubic than ever, charmed the first overworked waitress into bringing him crisp rashers, potatoes, kidneys, fresh toast, and coffee, looked at the clock and said something about five minutes to make the hangars, and then began to eat as if he had returned from a hunting expedition. 'Pretty whistled last night, boys,' he would say. 'Rather off my feed.'

He spent most of the rest of his life being brassed off. 'Good morning, Dibden,' you would say. 'How goes it?'

'Pretty much brassed off, old boy.'

'Oh, what's wrong?'

'Just brassed off, that's all. Just brassed off.'

This phrase, which, of course, was never in the papers either, covered all the troubles of Dibden's life. It covered all his troubles with his kite, his crew, his ops., his leave, his food, his popsie.

He was brassed off when ops. were on because of the increasing monotony of trying to prang the same target; he was brassed off when ops. were scrubbed because there was no target at all. He was brassed off because there was fog on the drome or because his popsie could not keep her date.

But however brassed off he was he succeeded in looking always the same: cherubic, grinning, bouncing, handsome, too irresponsible and altogether too like a schoolboy to be engaged in the serious business of flying an expensive bomber.

One afternoon Dibden was out over the coast of Holland on a daylight. It was his thirty-third trip: the veteran adding another four or five hours to his flying time. Down below, off the coast, he saw what he took to be an enemy tanker and he went down to have a look-see.

The tanker opened up at him with a fury of flak that surprised him, holing his port wing. I do not know what his emotions were, but I imagine that he was, simply, and as always, just brassed off. He went in and attacked the tanker with all he had, bombing first and then diving to machine-gun the deck.

The tanker hit back very hard, clipping a piece out of the starboard flap, but the more the tanker hit the more Dibden bounced back, like the ball thrown hard against the wall. His rear-gunner was very badly wounded, but Dibden still went in, firing with all he had left until the flak from the tanker ceased.

The next day there was in fact something about this in the papers. It did not sound very epic. 'Yesterday afternoon one of our bombers attacked a tanker off the Dutch coast. After the engagement the tanker was seen to be burning.'

It did not say anything about the holes in Dibden's wings or the way the outer port engine had cracked coming home. It did not in fact really say anything at all about that brief, bloody, and very bitter affair in which Dibden had bounced back repeatedly like an angry ball, or about the long journey home.

It did not say anything about Dibden landing on three engines with damaged flaps and a dying rear-gunner, or about a very tired, very brassed off Dibden coming in very late, with an unexpected hour on his flying-time, to boiled beef and tea.

Nor did it say anything about what happened that night. A little after midnight I came into the mess and there, under the bright lights of the ante-room, Dibden was doing some acrobatics. It was a very nice little party. At one end of the room two leather settees were placed endwise against each other, and then against them, endwise again, two chairs.

As I came in, Dibden, more cherubic, more smiling, more like a handsome Eskimo than ever, took a drink of light ale and then did a running somersault over the long line of furniture, landing with a wild whoop on his feet. His eyes were shining wildly. After him one or two other pilots tried it, but none of them was really good, and the only one who was good landed on his head. Then Dibden tried it again, and the fat, smiling ball of his body went over as easily as a bird.

Perhaps there was no connexion between the schoolboy Dibden joyfully throwing a somersault and the veteran Dibden angrily pranging a tanker. But as I saw Dibden hurling his fat little body into the air I felt suddenly that I understood all about his thirty-three trips, his golf-ball landings, his affair with the tanker, and the long, hard journey home. I understood why he flew, and why he flew as he did, and I understood the man he was.

But there was nothing about that, of course, in the papers.

How Sleep the Brave

THE SEA MOVED away below us like a stream of feathers smoothed down by a level wind. It was grey and without light as far as we could see. Only against the coast of Holland, in a thin line of trimming that soon lost itself in the grey coasts of the North, did it break into white waves that seemed to remain frozen between sea and land. Down towards Channel the sun, even from six thousand feet, had gone down at last below long layers of cloud. They had been orange and blue at first, then yellow and pale green, and then, as they were now, entirely the colour of slate. Above them there was nothing but a colourless sky that would soon be dark altogether.

There had been snow all over England that week. For two nights it had drifted against the huge wheels of the Stirling, in scrolls ten feet high. The wind had partially swept it from the smooth fabric of fuselages as it fell and then frost had frozen what remained of it into uneven drifts of papery dust. In the mornings gangs of soldiers worked at the runways, clearing them to black-white roads edged with low walls of snow, and lorries drove backwards and forwards along them, taking away like huge blocks of salt the carved-out drifts. In two more days the thaw came and yellow pools of snow-water lay in the worn places of the runways. It froze a little again late at night, leaving a muddy skin of ice on pools that looked dangerous with the sunlight level and cold on them in the early morning. It wasn't dangerous really and the wheels of the Stirlings smashed easily through the ice, splintering it like the silver glass toys on a Christmas tree. Then in the daytime the pools thawed again and if you watched the take-off from the control tower through a pair of glasses you saw the snow-water sparkle up from the wheels like brushes of silver feathers.

And now, beyond the hazy coast of Holland, with its thin white trimming that grew less white in the twilight as we flew towards it, we could see what reports had already told us. There was snow all over Europe. The day was too advanced to see it clearly. All you could see was a great hazy field of cotton-wool that had fewer marks on it than a layer of cloud. Far ahead of us, south and south-west and east, it ceased even to be white. It became the misty, colourless distances of all Europe, and suddenly as I looked at it, for almost the last time before darkness hit it altogether, I thought of what it would be like to fly on, southward, to the places I had never seen, the places without flak, the places in sunshine, the places beyond the war and the snow. It was one of those detached ideas that you get when flying, or rather that get you: a lightheaded idea that seems to belong to the upper air and is gone as soon as its futility has played with you.

For a few more minutes the trimming of coast lay dead below us and then, in a moment, was gone past us altogether. For just a few minutes longer the misty cotton-wool of the snow over Europe meant something, and then I looked and could see it no longer. Darkness seemed to have floated suddenly between the snow and the Stirling. What was below us was just negative. It was not snow, or land, or Europe. It was just the negative darkness that would flare any moment into hostility.

This darkness was to be ours for five hours or more. I was already cold and the aircraft was bumping like a goods train. The most violent bumps seemed to jerk a little more blood out of my feet. I remembered this sensation from other trips and now tried moving my toes in my boots. But the boots were too thick and my toes were already partially dead. This was my fifteenth trip as flight engineer but even now I could not get rid of two sensations that had recurred on all those trips since the very first: the feeling that I had no feet and the feeling, even more awful than that, that I had swallowed something horribly sour, like vinegar, which had now congealed between my chest and throat. I never thought of it as fear. I was always slightly scared, in a numb way, before the trips began, and before Christmas, before the snow fell, I had been more scared than hell on the Brest daylights. But now I only thought of this sourness as discomfort. It always did something to my power of speech. I always kept the inter-comm. mouthpiece ready, but I rarely used it. I could hear other voices over the inter-comm. but I rarely spoke, unless it was very necessary, in reply. It wasn't that I didn't want to speak, and it had little to do with the fact that Ellis, Captain of K. 42, did not encourage talking. I think I was scared that by speaking I might give the impression that I was scared. So I kept my mouth shut and let the sourness bump in my throat and pretended, as perhaps the other six of us pretended, that I was tough and taciturn and did not care.

'A lot of light muck on the port side, skipper.'

'O.K.'

The voice of Osborne, from the rear turret, came over the inter-comm., the Northern accent sharp and cold and almost an order in itself. Ossy, from Newcastle, five feet six, with the lean Newcastle face and grey monkey-wrinkled eyes, was the youngest of us. In battle-dress the wads of pictures in his breast pockets gave him a sort of oblong bust. In his Mae West this bust became quite big and handsome, so that he looked out of proportion, like a pouter pigeon. We always kidded Ossy about giving suck. But in his Mae West there was no room for his photographs; so always, before a trip, Ossy took them out and put them in his flying boots, one in each leg. In one leg of his boots he also carried a revolver, and in the other an American machine spanner. No one knew quite what this spanner was for, except perhaps that it was just one of those things that air-crews begin to carry about with them as foolish incidentals and that in the end become as essential as your right arm. So Ossy never came on trips except he had with him, in the legs of his boots, the things that mattered: the revolver, the spanner, and the pictures of a young girl, light-haired, print-frocked, pretty in a pale Northern way, taken in the usual back-garden attitudes on Tyneside. 'She's a wizard kid,' he said.

As for the spanner, if it was a talisman, I knew that Ed Walker, the second dickey, carried two rabbits' feet. You might have expected the devotion to a good-luck charm from Ossy, who anyway had the good sense to carry a spanner. But it surprised you that Winchester hadn't taught Ed Walker anything better than a belief in rabbits' feet. They were very ordinary rabbits' feet. The tendons had been neatly severed and the hair was quite neat and tidy and smooth. Ed kept them hidden under his shirts in a drawer in his bedroom and he didn't know that anyone knew they were there. I shared the room with him and one day when I opened the wrong drawer by mistake there were the rabbits' feet under the shirts, hidden as a boy might have hidden a packet of cigarettes from his father. Ed was very tall and slow-eyed and limp. He took a long time to dress himself and did not talk much. Between Winchester at eighteen and a Stirling at nineteen there wasn't much life to be filled in. He was so big that sometimes he looked lost; as if he had suddenly found himself grown up too quickly. And sometimes I used to think he didn't talk much solely for the reason that he hadn't much to say. But just because of that, and because of the rabbits' feet and the big lazy helplessness that went with them and because we could lie in bed and not talk much and yet say the right things when we did talk, we were fairly devoted.

Between the coast of Holland and the first really heavy German flak I always felt in a half-daze. I always felt my mind foreshorten its view. It was like travelling on a very long journey in a railway train. You didn't look forward to the ultimate destination, but only to the next station. In this way it did not seem so long. If it were night you could never tell exactly where you were, and sometimes you were suddenly surprised by the lights of a station.

We had no station lights: that was the only difference. We bumped on against the darkness. I don't know why I always felt it was against the darkness, and not in it or through it. Darkness on these long winter trips seemed to solidify. The power we generated seemed to cut it. We had to cut it to get through.

If we got through – but we did not say that except as a joke. At prayer-meeting, in intelligence room, before the trips, the Wing Commander always liked that joke. 'When you come back – *if* you come back.' But he was the only one, I think, who did like it, and most of us had given up laughing now. It might have been rather funnier if, for instance, he had said he hoped we had taken cases of light ale on board, or that we might get drunk on Horlick's tablets and black coffee. Not that this would have been very funny. And the funniest joke in the world, coming from him, wouldn't have given us any more faith than we had.

Faith is a curious thing to talk about. You can't put your hand on it, but there it is. And I think what we and that crew had faith in was not jokes or beam-approach or navigation or the kite itself, but Ellis.

'It's like a duck's arse back here,' Ossy suddenly said. 'One minute I'm in bloody Switzerland and the next I'm up in the North Sea.'

We laughed over the inter-comm.

'It's your ten-ton spanner,' Ellis said.

'What spanner, Skipper, what spanner?'

'Drop it overboard!'

'What spanner, what—'

'Go on, drop it. I can feel the weight of the bloody thing from here. You're holding us back.'

'There's flak coming up like Blackpool illuminations, Skip. Honest, Skip. Take plenty of evasive action—'

'Just drop the bloody spanner, Ossy, and shut up.'

We all laughed again over the inter-comm. There was a long silence, and then Ossy's voice again, now very slow:

'Spanner gone.'

We laughed again, but it was broken by the voice of Ellis. 'What about this Blackpool stuff?'

'It's all Blackpool stuff. Just like the Tower Ball-room on a carnival night.'

They were pumping it up all round us, heavy and light, and for a few minutes it was fairly violent. We were slapped about inside the kite like a collection of loose tools in a case.

Then from the navigation seat came the voice of Mac, the big Canadian from Winnipeg, slow and sardonic:

'Keep the milk warm, Ossy dear. It's baby's feed time.' And we laughed again.

After that, for a long time, none of us spoke again. I always noticed that we did not speak much until Ellis started the talk. The voice of Ellis was rather abrupt. The words were shot out and cut off like sections of metal ejected by a machine. I sometimes wondered what I was doing on these trips, in that kite, with Ellis, as flight engineer. He knew more about aero-engines generally, and about these aero-engines particularly, than I should ever know. If ever a man had a ground-crew devoted by the terror of knowledge it was Ellis.

We too were devoted by something of the same feeling. He was a small man of about thirty, a little younger than myself, with those large raw hands that mechanics sometimes have: the large, angular, metallic hands that seem to get their shape and power from the constant handling of tools. These hands, his voice, and finally his eyes were the most remarkable things about him. They were dark eyes that looked at you as impersonally as the lens of a camera. Before them you knew you had better display yourself as you were and not as you hoped you might be.

If Ed Walker had not begun to live, Ellis had lived enough for both of them. For so small a man it was extraordinary how far you had to look up to him, and I think perhaps we looked up at him because of the fullness of that life. A man like Ed would always be insular, clinging to the two neat rabbits' feet of English ideals. The sea, on which Ellis had served for five or six years before the war, had beaten the insularity out of him. It had given him the international quality of a piece of chromium. He was small but he gave out a feeling of compression. You had faith in him because time had tested the pressure his resistances could hold. He did not drink much: hardly at all. Most of us got pretty puce after bad trips, or good trips too if it comes to that, and sometimes people like Ossy got tearful in the bar of the Grenadier and looked wearily into the eyes of strangers and said 'We bloody near got wrapped up. Lost as hell. Would have been if it hadn't been for the Skipper,' and probably in the morning did not remember what they said.

But all of us knew that, and did remember. We knew too why Ellis did not drink. It was because of us. The sea, I think, had taught him something about the cold results of sobriety.

The flak was all the time fairly violent and now and then we dropped into pockets of muck that lifted the sourness acidly into my throat and dragged it down again through my stomach. It was always bad here. We were a good way over now and I remembered the met. reports at prayer-meeting: about seven-tenths over Germany and then clearing over the target. We had many bombers out that night and I hoped it would be clear.

Thinking of the weather, I went for a moment into one of those odd mesmeric dazes that you get on long trips, and thought of myself. I was the eldest of the crew: thirty, with a wife I did not live with now. I had been a successful under-manager in Birmingham and we had at one time a very nice villa on the outskirts. For some reason, I don't know why, we quarrelled a lot about little things like my not cleaning the bath after I'd used it, and the fact that my wife liked vinegar with salmon. We were both selfish in the same ways. We were like two beans that want to grow up the same pole and then strangle each other trying to do so. I had been glad of the war because it gave me the chance to break from her, and now flying had beaten some of the selfishness out of me. My self was no longer assertive. It had lost part of its identity, and I hoped the worst parts of its identity, through being part of the crew. It had done me good to become afraid of losing my skin, and my only trouble really was that I suffered badly from cold. I now could not feel my feet at all.

Suddenly I could not feel anything. Something hit us with a crack that seemed to lift us straight up as if we had been shot through a funnel. The shock tore me sideways. It flung me violently down and up and down again as if I had been a loose nut in a revolving cylinder.

II

'O.K. everybody?'

We had been shake like that before, on other trips, but never with quite that violent upward force. I lay on the floor of the aircraft and said something in answer to Ellis's voice. I hadn't any idea what it was. I wasn't thinking of myself, but only, at that moment, of the aircraft. I felt the blow had belted us miles upward, like a rocket.

I staggered about a bit and felt a little dazed. It seemed after a few moments that everybody was O.K. I looked at Mac, huge face immobile over the navigator's table, pinning down his charts and papers even harder with a violent thumb. I looked at his table and it was almost level. It did not tilt much with the motion of the aircraft and I knew then we were flying in a straight line. I looked at Allison, the radio operator, and his eyes, framed in a white circle between the earphones, looked back at me. He did not look any paler than usual. He did not look more fixed, more vacant, or more eaten up by trouble than usual. That was just the way he always looked. There had been a kind of cancerous emptiness on his face ever since a blitz had killed his child.

I grinned at him and then the next moment was not thinking of what had happened. The kite was flying well and I heard Ellis's voice again.

'Must be getting near, Mac?'

'About ten minutes, flying time.'

'O.K.'

She bumped violently once or twice as they spoke and seemed to slide into troughs of mud. The sick lump of tension bumped about in my throat and down into my bowels and up again.

'If I see so much as a flea's eyelash I'll feel bloody lucky,' Mac said.

He got up and began to grope his way towards the forward hatch. In those days the navigator did the bomb-aiming. Huge and ponderous and blown out, he looked in the dim light like the man in the adverts. for Michelin tyres. I sat down at his table. I felt sick and my head ached. Once as a boy, I had had scarlet fever and my head, as the fever came on, seemed to grow enormous and heavy, many times too large for my body. Now it was the same. It seemed like a colossal lump of helpless pulp on my shoulders. The light above the table seemed to flicker and splinter against my eyes.

I knew suddenly what it was. I wasn't getting my oxygen. It scared me for a moment and then I knew it must have been the fall. I don't quite know what I did. I must have fumbled about with the connexions for a time and succeeded in finding what was wrong at last.

I felt as if I began to filter slowly back into the aircraft. I came back with that awful mental unhappiness, split finally apart by relief, that you get as you struggle out of anaesthesia. I came back to hear the voices of Ellis and Mac, exchanging what I knew must be the instructions over the target. They seemed like disembodied voices. I tried to shake my brain into clarity. It seemed muddy and weak.

At last I got some sense into myself, but it was like exchanging one trouble for another. By the voices over the inter-comm. I knew that we had trouble. The weather was violent and sticky and Mac could not see. Something very dirty and unexpected had come up to change that serene met. forecast at prayer-meeting: clearing over the target. It was not clearing. We were in the middle of something violent, caught up by one of those sinister weather changes that make you hate wind and rain and ice with impotent stupidity.

'Try again, Skip? I can't see a bloody thing.'

'O.K. Again.'

Whether it cleared or not I never knew. Ellis took her in hand and it was something like driving a springless car down a mountain pass half blocked by the blast of rocks. We went in as steadily as that. The flak beat under the body of the aircraft and once or twice seemed to suck it aside. I held myself tense, throttling my whole body back. If all you needed was good insides and no capacity for thought I was only half equipped. I was not thinking, but my emotions had dissolved into my guts like water.

'Bombs gone!'

'O.K.' Ellis said. 'Thank Christ for that.'

A second later I felt the aircraft pull upwards, as if, bomb-less, she were suddenly more powerful than the weather. The force of that upward surge seemed to pull me together. It seemed to clean the heaving taste of oil and sickness out of my throat. I was glad too of the voice of Ellis, ejecting smoothly the repeated 'O.K. everybody?' We rocked violently, but I did not mind it. Whatever came now must be, I thought, an anti-climax to that moment. We had been in twice and out again. It was all that mattered now.

III

After two days' digging the rescue squad found the body of Allison's child, untouched but dead, pinned down into a cavity by a fallen door; and then Allison himself, his clothes plastered white as a limeworker's from the dust of debris washed by rain, crawled into the ruins and carried out the child in his own arms. She was still in her nightdress and she must have died as she was, the door falling but not striking her, making the little protective cavity, like a triangular coffin, in which she lay until they found her. Allison walked out of the bombed house and then, not knowing what he was doing, began to walk up the street, still carrying the child. He must have walked quite a long way, and quite fast, before anyone could stop him. He did not know what he was doing. He vaguely remembered a policeman and he remembered another man who took the child out of his arms. His idea was to take the child to his wife, who lay in hospital with a crushed shoulder and who had been crying out for the baby constantly for two days. He had an idea that it might help her if she saw the face of the child again.

It was my job among other things to watch the dials of the various engine pressures on the panel before me and to switch over the fuel tanks as and when it became necessary. On me depended, to a large extent, the balance of the aircraft. Sometimes you got a tank hit and the business of transferring the weight of fuel from one wing to another needed skill. There had been records of flight engineers who, in situations of this kind, and by their skill, had really brought an aircraft home.

I had never done anything as important as that and as I sat watching the dials on the panel I was thinking of Allison. You could never tell by his calm, white face what Allison was thinking. After the bomb had destroyed his house and child he had been away from the station for a couple of weeks. His wife got slowly better. He went back to see her quite often, for some days at a time, during the next six months. During this time he had fits of mutinous depression in which he wrote long letters to the boys, myself among them. They were always the same letters: the story of the child. He had nothing else to say because, obviously, there was nothing else in his life. He would always go back, for ever, to that moment; the moment when he carried the child from the house and up the street, himself like a dead person walking, until someone stopped him and took the child away. When he came back to operations with us he never once spoke of this; and none of us ever spoke of it either. I tried to understand for a time what Allison felt. Then I gave it up. I should have been surprised if he had felt anything at all. All that could be felt, whether it was fear or terror or anger or the mutilation of everything normal in you to utter despair, must have already been felt by Allison. He was inoculated for ever against terror and despair.

'Hell, it's the bloodiest night you ever saw,' Mac said.

'I could have told you that,' Thompson said. The voice of the sergeant in the mid-upper turret came over the inter-comm. 'And Skip., they'll have us in a bloody cone any minute.'

'God, it's dirty,' Mac said.

'They're heading for the straight,' Ossy said. 'Arse-end Charlie two lengths behind. Sergeant Thompson well up—'

'Stop nattering!' Ellis said.

We were hit a moment later. It was not so violent as the hit which had forced us upward, earlier, as in a funnel. It seemed like a colossal hand-clap. Terrific and shattering, it beat at us from both port and starboard sides. There was a moment as if you were in a vacuum. Then you were blown out of it. It was like the impact of an enormous and violent wave at sea.

I don't know what happened, but the next moment we were on fire. The flames made a noise like the hiss of a rocket before it leaves the ground. They shot with a slight explosive sound all along the port side of the fuselage, forward from where I sat. I yelled something through the inter-comm. and I heard Mac yelling too. I got hold of the fire extinguisher and began to work it madly. I remember the aircraft bumping so violently that it knocked my hands upward and I shot the extinguisher liquid on the roof. I fell down and got up again, still playing the extinguisher. Then I got the jet straight on to the flames and for a moment it transformed them into smoke, which began to fill the fuselage, so that we could not see. Then the flames shot up again. They blew outward suddenly and violently like the blow-back from a furnace. I felt them slap my face, scorching my eyeballs. Then I saw them shoot back and they ran fiercely up the window curtains. At that moment the extinguisher ran dry and I began to tear down the curtains with my bare hands, which were already numb with cold so that I could not feel the flames. I don't know quite what I did with those curtains. I must have beaten the flames out of them by banging them against my boots because I remember once looking down and seeing the sheepskin smouldering, and I remember how the idea of being on fire myself terrified me more than the idea of the 'plane itself being on fire.

Sometime before this the inter-comm. had gone and suddenly I saw Ellis, who until that moment could not have known much of what we were doing back there, open the door behind the pilot's seat. His face ejected itself and remained for a second transfixed, yellow beyond the smoke. I shall never forget it. I saw the mouth open and move, and I must have yelled something in reply before the door closed again. I had an awful feeling suddenly that Ellis had gone for ever. We were shut off, alone, with the fire, Mac and Allison and myself, and there was nothing Ellis could do.

All this time Allison sat there as if nothing was happening. You hear of wireless operators at sea, when the ship is sinking, having a kind of supernatural power of concentration. Allison had that concentration. Mac and I must have behaved like madmen. We hit the flames with the screwed-up curtains and with our bare hands and once I saw Mac press his huge Michelin body against the fuselage and kill the flames by pressure as he might have killed an insect on his back. The flames had a sort of maddening elasticity. It was like putting back the inner tube of a bicycle tyre. You pushed it back in one place and it leapt out again in another. Several times the aircraft rocked violently and we fell on the floor. When we got up again we fell against each other. All the time Allison sat there. And I knew that although it was amazing it was also right. He had to sit there. Somehow, if it killed us, we had to keep the flames from him. There was no room for three of us in the confined space of the fuselage, and it was the best thing that Allison should sit there, as if nothing had happened, clamped down by his earphones, as if in a world of his own. Allison was our salvation.

It was very hot by this time and suddenly I was very tired. I could not see very clearly. It was as if the blow-back of the flames had scorched the pupils of my eyes. They were terribly raw and painful, and the smoke seemed to soak into them like acid. I had no idea where we were. There were no voices in the inter-comm., but after a time the pilot's door opened and Ed Walker crawled back to Allison, with a written message. Allison read it and nodded. I tried to shout something at Ed, but I began to cough badly and it was useless. Then the flames broke out in two new places; on the port side, aft of where I had been sitting, and in the roof above my head. When I went to lift my hands to beat the flames they would not rise. It was like trying to lift the whole aircraft. I felt sick and the sickness ran weakly and coldly down the arteries of my arms and out of the fingers.

Then suddenly I made a great effort. I had been standing there helplessly for what seemed a long time. It could not have been more than a few seconds but it was like a gap of agony in a dream. I wanted to move but I could not move and so at last because I could not throw my hands against the flames I threw my whole body. I let it fall with outstretched arms against the fuselage and I felt the slight bounce of my Mae West as it hit the metal. I lay there for about a second, very tired. My head was limp against the hot metal of the fuselage and my eyes were crying from the acid of the smoke. Then I raised my head. I had come to the moment of not caring. The flames were burning my legs and I was too tired to beat them out again. I was going to burn and die and it did not matter.

Then I lifted my eyes. Shrapnel had torn a hole in the fuselage and I could just see at an angle through the gap. It was like looking out of a window and seeing out in the darkness the reflection of the fire in the room. It was only that this fire was magnified. It was like a huge level dish of flame. It was horizontal and the edges of it were torn to violent shreds in the night.

'Oh! Christ,' I said. 'Oh! Christ, Christ Jesus!'

I expected at any moment to see that burning wing tear past my face. It was fantastic to see it riding with us. It did not seem part of us. It was like an enormous orange and crimson torch sailing wildly through the darkness.

All the time I knew that it must split and break, that in a moment now we were at the end. And in some curious way the idea gave me strength. For the first time since the fire began I could think clearly. My hands and my mind were not tired. I thought of my helmet and took it off. The fire must have burnt a hole in the fuselage somewhere forward, for air was now blowing violently in, clearing a gulley through the smoke. I held my helmet and then swung it. The moment was very clear. The flames crawled like big yellow insects up the slope of the fuselage and I began to hit them, with a sort of delirious and final calm, with the helmet. At the same time I saw the faces of Mac and Allison. Mac too must have known about the fire on the wing. His eyes were big and protuberant with desperation. But Allison still sat there as if nothing had happened; thin, pale, his head manacled by the earphones.

Then something happened. It was Ed Walker, coming in through the pilot's door with a message. I saw him go to Allison and again I saw Allison nod his head. Then he beckoned us and we went to Allison's seat. Leaning over, we read the message. 'Over the sea. Take up ditching stations. Stand by for landing.' We were coming down.

I must have put my helmet back on my head. I must have strapped it quite carefully in the few seconds' interval between reading the message and beginning to haul out the dinghy. Then Ed Walker came back with Ossy, the rear-gunner, and then the mid-upper gunner climbed down. The five of us stood there, braced for about a minute. The fuselage was still burning and through the window the flat plate of flame along the wing had thickened and broadened and looked more fantastic than ever.

I stood braced and ready with the axe. I no longer felt tired and I knew that I might have to hit the door, if it jammed, with all the strength I had. As we came down, throttled back, but the speed violent still, I drew in my insides and held them so taut that they seemed to tie themselves in a single knot of pain.

Next moment we hit the water. And in that moment, as the violence of the impact lifted all of us upwards, I looked at Ossy. It was one of these silly moments that remained with me, clear and alive, long after the more confused moments of terror.

Ossy too was clenching something tightly in his hand. It was the spanner.

IV

K. 42 went down almost immediately, and except for a second or two when she was caught up in the light of her own fire, we never saw her again. I heard the port wing split with a crack before she went down, and I heard the explosive hiss of the sea beating over the flames. I could smell too the smell of fire and steam, dirty and hot and acid, blown at us on the wind. It remained in my mouth, sharp with the sourness of the sea-water, for a long time.

The next thing I knew was that we were in the dinghy. It was floating; it was right side up; and we were all there. I never knew at all how it happened. It was like a moment when, in a London raid, I had dived under a seat on a railway station. One moment I was standing waiting for the train; the next I was lying under the seat, my head under my arms, with a soldier and a girl. When I finally got up and looked under the seat it did not seem that there was room under it for a dog.

'Everybody O.K.?' Ellis said. 'I can't see you. Better answer your names.'

'I got a torch,' Mac said.

'O.K. Let's have a look at you.'

He shone the torch in our faces. The light burnt my eyes when I looked up.

'O.K. Everybody feel all right?'

'No, sir,' Ossy said. 'I'm bloody wet.'

We all laughed with extra heartiness at that.

'What was the last contact with base?'

'Half an hour before we hit the drink,' Allison said.

'You think they got you?'

'They were getting me then,' Allison said. 'But afterwards we were off course. The transmitter was u.s. after the fix.'

'All right,' Ellis said. 'And listen to me.' He shone the torch on his wrist. 'It's now eleven ten. I'm going to call out the time every half-hour.'

The torch went out. It seemed darker than ever. The dinghy rocked on the sea.

'Remember what the wind was, Mac?'

'She was north north-east,' Mac said. 'About thirty on the ground.'

'Any idea where we should be?'

'We were on course until that bloody fire started. But Jesus, you did some evasive action after that. Christ knows where we went.'

'We ought to be in the North Sea somewhere, just north-west of Holland.'

'I guess so,' said Mac.

'North north-east – that might blow us down-Channel.'

'In time it might blow us to Canada,' Mac said.

'As soon as it gets light we can get the direction of the wind,' Ellis said. 'We'll use the compass and then you'll all paddle like hell.'

I sat there and did not say anything. I knew now that my hands were burnt, but I did not know how badly. I tried putting them in my pockets, but with the rocking of the dinghy I could not balance myself. The pain of my hands all that night was my chief concern. The pain of my eyes, which were scorched too, did not seem so bad. I could shut them against the wind, and for long intervals I did so, riding on the dinghy blindly, the swell of the wave magnified because I could not see. It was better to close my eyes. If I did so the wind, cold and steady but not really strong, could not reach the raw eyeballs. The sea-spray could not hit them and pain them any more.

But I could not shut my hands. Fire seemed to have destroyed the reflex action of the muscles. The fingers stood straight out. It was not so much the pain of burning as the pain of a paralysis in which the nerves had been stripped raw. I had to hold them in one position. In whatever way my body moved my hands remained outstretched and stiff. When the sea broke over the dinghy, as it did at the most unexpected moments, the spray splashed my hands and the salt was like acid on the burns and I could not dry it off. I had to sit there until the wind dried it for me. And then it was as if the wind was freezing every spit of spray into a flake of ice and that the flakes were burning my hands all over again.

I sat there all night, facing the wind. Every half-hour Ellis gave out the time. He said nothing about rations or about the rum. From this I gathered that he was not hopeful about our position. It seemed to mean that he expected us to be a long time in the dinghy and that we must apportion rations for two, three, or perhaps four days. I had noticed too that all through the period of snow, for the last week, the wind rose steadily with the sun. By mid-afternoon, on land, it blew at forty or fifty miles an hour, raising white frozen dust in savage little clouds on the runways. Then it dropped with the sun. So if in the morning the wind strengthened we should, I thought, have a hard job to paddle crossways against it; which was our way to England. We should drift towards the Channel, into the Straits, and then down-Channel. Nothing could stop us.

The wind would be strongest when we could paddle best, and weakest when we could not steer well. I saw that we might drift for days and end up, even if we were lucky, far down the French coast, certainly not east of Cherbourg. I did not see how we could reach England.

Perhaps it did me good to think like this. I know that afterwards Ellis thought much like it; except that he had a worse fear – that we might be so near the coast of Europe that, that night before we could realize our position, we might be blown into the shore of Germany or Holland. It was at least better than thinking like Ossy, who seemed so sure he would be in England in the morning and in Newcastle, on crash leave, in the afternoon.

And to think of this kept me from thinking of my hands. My mind, thinking of the possibility of future difficulties, went ahead of my pain. All night, too, there was little danger from the sea. It was very cold but the dinghy rode easily, if rather sluggishly, in the water. Our clothes were very wet and I could feel the water slapping about my boots in the well of the dinghy. We simply road blindly in the darkness, without direction, under a sky completely without stars and on a sea completely without noise except for the flat slapping of waves on the rubber curve of the dinghy.

After a time I managed to bandage my hands very roughly with my handkerchief. The handkerchief was in my left trousers-pocket. I could not stand up or, in the confined space of the well that was full of feet, move my leg more than a few inches. But at last I straightened my thigh downward a little, and then my left hand downward against my thigh. The pain of touching the fabric filled my mouth with sickness. It was like pushing your hand into fire. When I pushed my hand still further down the sickness dried in my mouth and the roof of it and my tongue were dry and contracted, as if with alum. Then I pushed my hand further down. I could just feel the handkerchief between the tips of my fingers. I drew it out very slowly. The opening of the pocket, chafing against my hand, seemed to take off the flesh. The raw pain seemed to split my hand and long afterwards, when my hands were covered by the handkerchief and warm and almost painless, my head was cold with the awful sweat of pain.

I sat like that for the rest of the night, my hands roughly bound together.

V

We were all quite cheerful in the morning. The sky in the east was split into flat yellow bars of wintry light. As they fell on the yellow fabric of the dinghy it looked big and safe and friendly. The wind was not strong and the air no colder. The sea was everywhere the colour of dirty ice.

Ellis then told us what our position was.

'I am dividing the rations for three days,' he said. I knew afterwards that this was not true. He was reckoning on their lasting for six days. 'We eat in the morning. You get a tot of rum at midday. Then a biscuit at night. That's all you'll get.'

We did not say anything.

'Now we paddle in turns, two at a time, fifteen minutes each. If the wind is still north north-east it means steering at right angles across it. We can soon check the wind when the sun comes up. It ought to come almost behind the sun. It means paddling almost north. The risk is that we'll bloody well go down-Channel and never get back.'

None of us said anything again.

'I'll dish the rations out and then we'll start. We'll start with a drop of rum now, because it's the first time. Then Ossy and Ed start paddling; then Mac and Ally; then Thompson and – what's the matter with your hands?' he said to me.

'Burnt a bit,' I said.

'Can you hold anything?'

'They won't reflex or anything,' I said. 'But my wrists are all right. I could hold the paddle with my wrists.'

'Don't talk cock!' he said.

'I can't sit here doing nothing,' I said.

'O.K.,' he said, 'you can call out the time. Every hour now. And anyway it'll take us an hour to bandage those hands.'

Ossy and Ed started paddling. They were fresh and paddled rather raggedly at first, over-eager, one long-armed and one short so that the dinghy rocked.

'Take it steady,' Ellis said. 'Keep the sun on your right cheek. Take long strokes. You've got all day.'

'Not if I know it,' Ossy said. 'I got crash-leave coming, so I'll catch the midnight to Newcastle.'

'You've got damn all coming if you don't keep your mouth shut. Do you want your guts full of cold air?'

Ellis got out his first-aid pack and peeled off the adhesive tape. He had changed places with Thompson and was sitting next to me.

'What did you do?' he said .'Try to fry yourself?'

'I dropped my gloves,' I said.

'Take it easy,' he said. 'I'll take the handkerchief off.'

He took off the handkerchief and for some moments I could not move my hands. The air seemed to burn again the shining swollen blisters. I sat in a vacuum of pain. Oh! Christ, I thought. Oh, Jesus, Jesus! I fixed my eyes on the horizon and held them there, blind to everything except the rising and falling line below the faint yellow bars of sun. I held my hands raw in the cold air and the wind savagely drove white-hot needles of agony down my fingers. Jesus, I thought, please, Jesus. I knew I could not bear it any more and then I did bear it. The pain came in waves that rose and fell with the motion of the dinghy. The waves swung me sickeningly up and down, my hands part of me for one second and then no longer part of me, the pain stretching away and then driving back like hot needles into my naked flesh.

I became aware after a time of a change of colour in the sea. This colour travelled slowly before my eyes and spewed violently into the dinghy. It was bright violet. I realized that it seemed one moment part of the sea and one moment part of the dinghy because it was, in reality, all over my hands. The motion of the dinghy raised it to the line of sea and spewed it down into the yellow wall of fabric.

I was not fully aware of what was happening now. I knew that the violet colour was the colour of the gentian ointment Ellis was squeezing on my hands; I knew that the pure whiteness that covered it was the white of bandage. For brief moments my mind was awake and fixed. The violet and white and yellow and the grey of the sea were confused together. They suddenly became black and the blackness covered me.

When I could look at the sea again and not see those violent changes of colour the sun was well above the horizon and Mac and Allison were paddling. I did not then know they were paddling for the second time. I held my hands straight out, the wrists on my knees, and stared at the sea. It was roughened with tiny waves like frosted glass. I did not speak for a long time and the men in the dinghy did not speak to me. There was no pain in my hands now. And in my mind the only pain was the level negative pain of relief, the pain after pain, that had no violence or change.

I must have sat there all morning, not speaking. We might

have drifted into the coast and I shouldn't have known it. I watched the sun clear itself of the low cloud lying above the sea, and then the sky itself clear slowly about the sun. It became a pale wintry blue and as the sun rose the sea was smoothed down, until it was like clean rough ice as far as you could see.

It must have been about midday that I was troubled with the idea that I ought to paddle. From watching the sea I found myself watching the faces of the others. They looked tired in the sun. I realized that I had been sitting there all morning, doing nothing. I did not know till afterwards that I had called out the time, from the watch on my wrist, every hour.

But now I wanted to paddle. I had to paddle. I had to pull my weight. It seemed agonizing and stupid to sit there, not moving or speaking, but only watching with sore and half-dazed eyes that enormous empty expanse of sea and sky. I had to do something to break the level pain of that monotony.

Thinking this, I must have tried to stand up.

'Sit down, you bloody fool! Sit down!' Ellis yelled. 'Sit down!'

The words did not hurt me. I must have obeyed automatically, not knowing it. But in the second that Ellis shouted I was myself again. The stupefaction of pain was broken. For the first time since daybreak I looked at the men about me. They ceased being anonymous. I really saw their faces. They were no longer brown-yellow shapes, vague parts of the greater yellow shape of the dinghy. They were the men I knew, and I was consciously and fully with them, alive again.

'You feel better?' Ellis said.

'I'm all right.'

'I gave you a shot,' he said.

'I'm all right. I could paddle.'

'You could bloody hell,' he said.

'I could do something,' I said. 'I want to do something.'

'O.K. Keep a look-out. Bawl as soon as you see anything that looks like a kite or a sail.'

From that moment I felt better. I could not use my hands, but I had something on which to use my eyes. The situation in the morning had seemed bad. Now I turned it round. There was nothing so bad that it couldn't be worse. Supposing my eyes had been burnt out, and not my hands? I felt relieved and grateful and really quite hopeful now.

At one o'clock exactly we had a small tot of rum. The wind had risen, as I thought it would with the sun. But there was no cloud and no danger, that afternoon, of snow. Visibility was down to two or three miles and in the far distance there was a slight colourless haze on the face of the sea. But it was, as far as you could tell, good flying weather.

'So,' as Ellis said, 'there is a chance of a patrol. The vis. isn't improving, but it ought to be good enough. It all depends anyway on the next two hours.'

No one paddled as we drank the rum. We rested for ten minutes. Then Ossy and Ed began paddling again. Helped by the rest, the rum, and the fact that the sun was so clear and bright on the water, we all felt much more hopeful. Occasionally a little water swilled over into the dinghy, but the next moment Allison, calm and methodical, baled it out again with his hands.

I kept watching the sea and the sky. At two o'clock I called out the time. The hour seemed to have gone very quickly. I realized that we had one more hour in which we could hope to be seen by an aircraft; only two in which we could hope, even remotely, to be picked up. But I was not depressed. I do not think any of us were depressed. It was good that we were together, dependent, as we always had been, on each other. And we were so far only looking forward, not backward. We had no disappointment to feed on, but only the full hope of the afternoon. None of us knew that Ellis had already prepared himself, as early as one o'clock, for another night in the dinghy.

It must have been about half-past two when Allison shouted. He began waving his hands, too. It was the most excitable Allison I had ever seen, his hands waving, and his head thrown backward in the sun.

'You see it?' he shouted. 'You see it?'

I saw the kite coming from north-westwards, about right angles to the sun. It was black and small, and flying at about six thousand.

'It's a single-engine job,' Ossy said.

'A Spit,' Thompson said.

She came towards us level and straight, not deviating at all. I felt the excitement pump into my throat. She seemed to be about a mile or two away and was coming fast. It was not like the approach of a ship. In a few seconds she would pass over us; she would go straight on or turn. It would be all over in a few seconds. 'Come on, baby,' Mac said. 'For Pete's sake don't you know you got too much altitude? Come on, baby,' he whispered, 'blast and damn you, come on.'

We had ceased paddling. The dinghy rocked slowly up and down. As the Spitfire came dead over us our seven faces must have looked to its pilot, if he had seen us at all, like seven empty white plates on the rim of a yellow table. They must have looked for one second like this before they tilted slowly down, and then finally upside down as we stared at our feet in the well of the dinghy.

'He'll be back,' Ossy said. 'He's bound to come back.'

None of us spoke in answer, and it was some time after I heard the last sound of the 'plane that Mac and Allison began paddling again.

VI

The 'plane did not come back and the face of the sea began to darken about four o'clock. From the colour of slate on the western horizon the sunset rose through dirty orange to cold pale green above. The wind had almost dropped with the sun and except for the slap of the paddles hitting the water there was no sound.

Soon Ellis ordered the paddling to cease altogether. Then we sat for about half an hour between light and darkness, the dinghy rocking sluggishly up and down, and ate our evening meal.

To each of us Ellis rationed out one biscuit and one piece, about two inches square, of plain chocolate. I could not hold either the biscuit or the chocolate in my hands, which Ellis had covered with long white muffs of bandage. Ellis therefore held them for me, giving me first a bite of chocolate, then a bite of the biscuit. I ate these very slowly, and in between the mouthfuls Ellis did something to my hands. 'If she comes rough in the night you may get them wet,' he said.

In the morning Ellis had saved the fabric of the first-aid pack and the adhesive tape that bound the biscuit tin. Now he undid another pack and put the bandages and the ointments and the lint inside his Mae West. Then with the two pieces of fabric he made bags for my hands. I put my hands into these bags and Ellis bound them about my wrists with the adhesive tape. It was a very neat job and I felt like a boxer.

'Now we'll work the night like we did the paddling,' he said. 'We'll split it into one-hour watches with two on a watch.'

He gave me the last of the chocolate before he went on speaking. It clung to the roof of my mouth and I felt very thirsty. Below the taste of the chocolate there was still a faint taste, dry and acrid, of the burning 'plane.

'Ed and Ossy begin from five o'clock. Then Ally and Mac. Then Thompson and myself.'

'What about me?' I said. 'I'm all right.'

'You've got your work cut out with your hands,' he said.

'I'm O.K.,' I said.

'Look after your hands,' he said. 'And don't go to sleep. You're liable to get bounced off this thing before the night's gone.'

You did not argue with Ellis when the tone of his voice was final. Now it was very final and without answering I sat watching the western sky. It was colourless and clear now, with the first small stars, quite white, beginning to shine in the darker space about the sunset. I don't know how the others felt about these stars or if they noticed them at all, but they gave me a sense of comfort. I was determined not to be downcast. I was even determined not to be hopeful. My hands did not seem very bad now and I felt no colder than I had always been. I knew we should not be picked up that night; or even perhaps the next day. So as darkness came on and the stars increased until they were shining so brightly that I could see the reflection of the largest of them brokenly tossed like bits of phosphorescence in the sea, I did as I had always done on a long trip to Germany. I foreshortened the range of my thoughts. I determined not to think beyond the next hour, when the watch would be changed.

Being in that dinghy, that night, not knowing where we were or where we were going, all of us a little scared but all of us too scared to show it, was rather like having an operation. It smoothed the complications of your life completely. Before the operation the complication from all sorts of causes, small and large, income tax, unanswered letters, people you hated, people who hurt you, bills, something your wife said about your behaviour, seemed sometimes to get your life into an awful mess. Many things looked like small catastrophes. It was a catastrophe if you were late at the office, or if you couldn't pay a bill. Then suddenly you had to have your operation. And in a moment nothing mattered except one thing. The little catastrophes were cancelled out. All your life up to the moment of lying on the stretcher dissolved away, smoothed and empty of all its futilities and little fears. All that mattered was that you came through.

My attitude on the dinghy that night became like that. Before the moment we had taken off, now more than a day ago, and had flown out towards the snows of Europe, there was little of my life that seemed to matter. You hear of people cast away in open boats who dream sadly of their loved ones at home. But I didn't dream of anyone. I felt detached and in a way free. The trouble with my wife – whether we could make a go of it or whether we really hated each other or whether it was simply the strain of the war – no longer mattered. All my life was centred into a yellow circle floating without a direction on a dark sea.

It must have been about midnight when we saw, in what we thought was the east, light fires breaking the sky in horizon level. They were orange in colour and intermittent, like stabs of Morse. We knew that it was light flak somewhere on a coast, but which coast didn't really trouble us. The light of that fire, too far away to be heard or reflected in the dark sea, comforted us enormously.

We watched it for more than two hours before it died away. Looking up from the place where the fire had been and into the sky itself, I realized that the stars had gone. I remember how the sudden absence of all light, first the far-off flak, then the stars, produced an effect of awful loneliness. It must then have been about three o'clock. During the time we were watching the flak we had talked a little, talking of where we thought it was. Now, one by one, we gave up talking. Even Ossy gave up talking, and once again there was no sound except the slapping of the sea against the dinghy

But about an hour later there was a new sound. It was the sound of the wind rising and skimming viciously off the face of the sea, slicing up glassy splinters of spray. And there was now a new feeling in the air with the rising of the wind.

It was the feeling of ice in the air.

VII

When day broke, about eight o'clock, we were all very cold. Our beards stood out from our faces and under the bristles the skin was shrunk. Mac, who was very big, looked least cold of all; but the face of Allison, thin and quite bloodless, had something of the grey whiteness of broken edges of foam that split into parallel bars the whole face of the sea. This grey-whiteness made Allison's eyes almost black and they sank deep into his head. In the same way the sea between the bars of foam had a glassy blackness too.

The wind was blowing at about forty miles an hour and driving us fairly fast before it. The sky was a grey mass of ten-tenths cloud, so thick that it never seemed to move in the wind. Because there was no sun I could not tell if the wind had changed. I knew only that it drove at your face with an edge of raw ice that seemed to split the skin away.

Because of this coldness Ellis changed his plans.

'It's rum now and something to eat at midday. Instead of the other way round.'

As we each took a tot of rum Ellis went on talking.

'We'll paddle as we did yesterday. But it's too bloody cold

to sit still when you're not paddling. So you'll all do exercises to keep warm. Chest-slapping and knee-slapping and any other damn thing. It's going to get colder and you've got to keep your circulation.'

He now gave us, after the rum, a Horlick's tablet each.

'And now any suggestions?'

'It's sure bloody thing we won't get to Newcastle at this rate,' Ossy said.

'You're a genius,' Ellis said.

'Couldn't we fix a sail, Skip?' Ossy said. 'Rip up a parachute, or even use a whole chute?'

'How are you going to hold your sail?' Ellis said. 'With hay-rakes or something?'

All of us except Allison made suggestions, but they were not very good. Allison alone did not speak. He was always quiet, but now he seemed inwardly quiet. He had scarcely any flesh on his face and his lips were blue was if bruised with cold.

'O.K., then,' Ellis said. 'We carry on as we did yesterday. Ossy and Ed start paddling. The rest do exercises. How are your hands?' he said to me.

'O.K.,' I said. I could not feel them except in moments when they seemed to burn again with far-off pain.

'All right,' he said. 'Time us again. A quarter of an hour paddling. And if the sea gets worse there'll have to be relays of baling too.'

When Ossy and Ed started paddling I saw why Ellis had talked of baling. The dinghy moved fast and irregularly; it was hard to synchronize the motions of the two paddles when the sea was rough. We were very buoyant on the sharp waves and sometimes the crests hit us sideways, rocking us violently. We began to ship water. It slapped about in the well of the dinghy among our seven pairs of feet. It hit us in the more violent moments on the thighs and even as far up as our waists. We were so cold that the waves of spray did not shock us and except when they hit our faces we did not feel them. Nevertheless I began to be very glad of the covers Ellis had put on my hands.

Soon all of us were doing something: Ossy and Ed paddling; Thompson and Ellis baling out the water, Thompson with a biscuit tin, Ellis with a small tobacco tin. They threw the water forward with the wind. While these four were working Mac and Allison did exercises, beating their knees and chests with their hands. Mac still looked very like the Michelin tyre advertisement, huge, clumsy, unsinkable. To him the exercises were a great joke. He beat his knees in dance time, drumming his hands on them. It kept all of us except Allison in good spirits. But I began to feel more and more that Allison was not there with us. He slapped his knees and chest with his hands, trying to keep time with Mac, but there was no change in his face. It remained vacant and deathly; the dark eyes seemed driven even deeper into the head. It began to look more and more like a face in which something had killed the capacity for feeling.

We went on like this all morning, changing about, two exercising, two paddling, two baling out. The wind did not rise much and sometimes there were moments when it combed the sea flat and dark. The waves, short and unbroken for a few moments, then looked even more ominous. Then with a frisk of the wind they rose into fresh bars of foam.

It was about midday when I saw the face of the sea combed down into that level darkness for a longer time than usual. The darkness travelled across it from the east, thickening as it came. Then as I watched, it became lighter. It became grey and vaporous, and then for a time grey and solid. This greyness stood for a moment a mile or two away from us, on the sea, and then the wind seemed to fan it to pieces. These millions of little pieces became white and skimmed rapidly over the dark water, and in a moment we could not see for snow.

The first thing the snow did was to shut out the vastness of the empty sea. It closed round us, and we were blinded. The area of visible sea was so small that we might have been on a pond. In a way it was comforting.

Those who were paddling went on paddling and those who were baling went on baling the now snow-thickened water. We did not speak much. The snow came flat across the sea and when you opened your mouth it drove into it. I bent my head against it and watched the snow covering my hands. For the last hour they had begun to feel jumpy and swollen and God knew what state they were in.

It went on snowing like that for more than an hour, the flakes, big and wet and transparent as they fell. They covered the outer curve of the dinghy, on the windward side, with a thick wet crust of white. They covered our bent backs in the same way, so that we looked as if we were wearing white furs down to our waists, and they thickened to a yellow colour the sloppy water in the dinghy.

All the time Allison was the only one who sat upright. At first I thought he was being clever; because he did not bend his back the snow collected only on his shoulders. That seemed a good idea. Then, whenever I looked up at him, I was struck by the fact that whether he was paddling or baling his attitude was the same. He sat stiff, bolt upright, staring through the snow. His hands plunged down at his side automatically, digging a paddle into the water, or scooping the water out of the dinghy and baling it away. His eyes, reflecting the snow, were not dark. They were cold and colourless. He looked terribly thin and terribly tired, and yet not aware of being tired. I felt he had simply got into an automatic state, working against the sea and the snow, and that he did not really know what he was doing. Still more I felt that he did not care.

I knew the rest of us cared very much. After the first comfortable shut-in feeling of the snow had passed we felt desperate. I hated the snow now more than the sea. It shut out all hope that Air-Sea Rescue would ever see us now. I knew that it might snow all day and I knew that after it, towards sunset, it would freeze. If it snowed all day, killing all chances of rescue, and then froze all night, we should be in a terrible state the next morning, our third day.

The thought of this depressed me, for a time, very much. It was now about half-past twelve. The time seemed crucial. Unless it stopped snowing very soon, so that coastal stations could sent out patrols in the early afternoon, we must face another night on the dinghy. I knew that all of us, with the exception of Allison, felt this. We were very tired and cold and stiff from not stretching our bodies, and the snow, whirling and thick and wet, seemed to tangle us up into a circle from which we were never going to get out.

In such moments as this Ellis did the right thing. He had driven us rather hard all morning, getting us out of small depressed moments by saying: 'Come on, we've got to keep going. Come on,' or with a dry joke, 'No fish and chips for Ossy if we don't keep going. It's tough tit for Ossy if he doesn't get his fish and chips.' He knew just when he could drive us no longer. Now he let up.

'O.K.,' he said. 'Give it a rest.'

'Holy Moses,' Mac said. 'I used to love snow. Honest, I used to love the bloody stuff.'

Even Mac looked tired. The snow had collected on his big head, giving him the look of an old man with white hair.

'Jesus,' he said. 'I'll never feel the same way about snow again.'

'What time do you make it?' Ellis said to me.

'Twelve forty-five coming up to six – now,' I said.

'O.K.,' he said. 'Set your watches.'

While we set our watches, synchronizing them, calling out the figures, Ellis got out the rum, the chocolate and the biscuits. Afterwards I looked back and knew it was not so much the food, as Ellis's order to synchronize the watches, that made me feel better at that moment. Time was our link with the outside world. From setting our watches together we got a sense of unity.

Ellis gave out the chocolate and the biscuits, in the same ration as before.

'Everybody all right? Ossy?'

'I'm a bloody snowball, if that's anything,' Ossy said.

'Good old Ossy.'

Ellis looked at each of us in turn. 'All right, Ally?' he said.

Allison nodded. He still sat bolt upright and he still did not speak.

Ellis did not speak either until it was time to tot out the rum. He used the silver bottom of an ordinary pocket-flask for the rum and this, about a third full, was our ration. He always left himself till last, but this time he did not drink. 'God, I always hate the stuff. It tastes like warm rubber,' he said.

'Drink it, Ally,' he said.

Allison held out his hand. I could see that the fingers were so cold that, like my own after the burning, they would not flex. I saw Ellis bend them and fold them, like a baby's, over the tot. I saw the hand remained outstretched, stiff in the falling snow, until finally Allison raised it slowly to his lips. I think we all expected to see that cup fall out of Allison's hands, and we were all relieved and glad when at last Ellis reached over and took it away.

As we sat there, rocking up and down, there was a slight lessening of the snow. Through the thinning flakes we could see, soon, a little more of the sea. No sooner could I see more of it than I hated it more. I hated the long troughs and the barbarous slits of foam between them and the snow driving, curling and then flat, like white tracer above. I hated the ugliness and emptiness of it and above all the fact of its being there.

VIII

That afternoon a strange thing happened. By two o'clock the snow grew thinner and drew back into a grey mist that receded over the face of the sea. As it cleared away altogether the sky cleared too, breaking in a southerly direction to light patches of watery yellow which spread under the wind and became spaces of bright blue. Across these spaces the sun poured in musty shafts and the inner edges of cloud were white than the snow had been. Far off, below them, we saw pools of light on the sea.

We were now paddling roughly in a straight line away from the sun. We were all, with the exception of Allison, quite cheerful. There was something tremendously hopeful about this breaking up of the sky after snow.

Allison alone sat there as if nothing had happened. He had not spoken since morning. He still looked terribly cold and tired and yet as if he did not know he was tired.

Suddenly he spoke.

'Very lights,' he said.

'Hell!' Mac said. 'Where?'

'Look,' Allison said.

He was pointing straight before us. The sky had not broken much to the north and the cloud there was very low.

'I don't see a bloody thing,' Mac said.

'Christ, if it is,' Ossy said. 'Christ, if it is.'

We were all very excited. The paddling and baling stopped, and we rocked in the water.

'Where did you see this?' Ellis said.

'There,' Allison said. He was still pointing, but his eyes were as empty as they had always been.

'You're sure they were Very lights?'

'I saw them.'

'How long were they burning?'

'They just lit up and went out.'

'But where? Where exactly?'

'You see the dark bit of cloud under there? They came out of that.'

We all looked at that point for a long time. I stared until my eyeballs seemed to smart with hot smoke again.

'Ally, boy,' Mac said. 'You must have awful good eyesight.'

'What would Very lights be doing at this time of day?' Ed said.

'I can't think,' Ellis said. 'Probably Air-Sea Rescue. It's possible. They'd always be looking.'

'A kite wouldn't be dropping them unless it saw something.'

'It might. Funny things happen.'

'Hell they do,' Mac said.

'You couldn't expect even Air-Sea Rescue to see us in this muck,' I said.

Ossy and Ed began to paddle again. As we went forward we still kept our eyes on the dark patch of cloud, but nothing happened. Nor did Allison speak again; nor had any of us the heart to say we thought him mistaken.

For a time we hadn't the heart for much at all. The situation in the dinghy now looked messy and discouraging. The melting snow was sloppy in the bottom, a dirty yellow colour; there were too many feet. It was still very cold and when we tried to do exercises – I could only beat my elbows against my sides – we knocked clumsily against each other. We had done that before, in the morning, and once or twice it had seemed mildly funny. Now it was more irritating than the snow, the cold and the disappointment of Allison's false alarm.

All this time the sky was breaking up. In the west and south, through wide blue lakes of cloud, white shafts of sun fell as bright and cold as chromium on the sea. These shiny edges of sunlight sometimes produced a hallucination. They looked in the distances like very white cliffs, jagged and unbelievably real. Staring at them, it was easy to understand why Allison had seen a Very light in a cloud.

So we paddled until three o'clock; and I knew it was hopeless. We had another hour of daylight: the worst of the day. The sea, with the sun breaking on it, looked terribly empty; but with the darkness on it we should at least having nothing to look for. Ellis, as always, was very good at this moment. His face was red and fresh and his eyes, bright blue, did not look very tired. He had managed somehow to keep neater than the rest of us. You felt he had kept back enormous reserves of energy and hope and that he hadn't even begun to think of the worst. And now he suddenly urged us to sing. 'Come on, a sing-song before tea, chaps,' he said. 'Come on.'

So we began singing. We first sang 'Shenandoah' and 'Billy Boy'. Then we sang other songs, bits of jazz, and 'Daisy, Daisy', and then we came back to 'Shenandoah'. We sang low and easy and there was no resonance about it because of the wind. But it was a good thing to sing because you could sing the disappointment out of yourself and it kept you from thinking. We must have gone on singing for nearly an hour and the only one of us who didn't sing much was Allison. From time to time I saw his mouth moving. It simply moved up and down, rather slowly, erratically, out of tune. Whatever he was singing did not belong to us. He was very pale and the cavity of his mouth looked blue and his eyes were distant and dark as if they were still staring at those Very lights in the distant cloud.

It must have been about four o'clock when he fell into the dinghy. The sea pitched us upward and Allison fell forward on his face. He fell loosely and his head struck the feet crowded in the bottom of the dinghy, which rocked violently with the fall.

Ellis and Mac pulled him upright again. His face was dirty with snow water and his eyes were wide open. Ellis began to rub his hands. The veins on the back of them were big and blue, the colour of his lips, and he began to make a choking noise in his throat. His body was awkward and heavy in the well of the dinghy and it was hard to prevent him from slipping down again. The dinghy rocked badly and I thought we might capsize.

'Put him between my knees,' I said. 'I can hold him like that.'

They propped him up and I locked his body with my knees, keeping it from falling. I held my bandaged hands against his face and he made a little bubbling noise with his mouth, not loud, but as if he was going to be gently sick.

As I held him like that and as we bumped about in the dinghy, badly balanced, swinging and rocking like one of those crazy boats at a fun fair, I looked at the sky.

The sun had suddenly gone down. Already above the sunset the sky was clear and green and I could feel the frost in the air.

IX

I held Allison's body with my knees all that night and his face with my damaged hands. My legs are long and gradually the feeling went out of them. But once I had got into that position it was too complicated to move.

As darkness came down ice began to form like thin rough glass on the outer sides of the dinghy, where the snow had first settled and thawed. Frost seemed to tighten up the rubber, which cracked off the ice as it moved with the waves. It was bitterly cold, very clear and brittle, without much wind. The sky was very clear too and there was a splintering brightness in the stars.

At intervals of about an hour we gave Allison drinks of rum. At these moments he did not speak. He would make the gentle, bubbling noise with his lips and then leave his mouth open, so that a little of the rum ran out again. I would shut his mouth with my hand. Sometimes I put my unbandaged wrists on his face and it was as cold as stone.

All that night, in between these times, I thought a lot. The cold seemed to clear my brain. All the feeling had gone from my hands and from my legs and thighs, and my head seemed almost the only part of me alive. For the first time I thought of what might be happening, or what might yet happen, at home. I thought of base, where they would be wondering about us. I could see the Mess ante-room: the long cream room with the fire at one end, the pictures of Stirlings on the walls, the chaps playing cards, someone drumming to a Duke Ellington record on the lid of the radio. I wondered if they had given us up. I wondered too about the papers. If they had already said anything about us it could only be in the dead phrase: one of our aircraft is missing. Hearing it, did anyone think about it again? We had been drifting for two days on the sea and for a long time we had been on fire in the air. If we didn't come back no one would ever know. If we did come back the boys at the station would be glad, and perhaps the papers would give us a line in a bottom corner. I didn't feel very bitter but that night, as I sat there, holding Allison with my burnt hands, I saw the whole thing very clearly. We had been doing things that no one had ever done before. Almost every week you read of aircraft on fire in the air. You read it in the papers and then you turned over and read the sports news. You heard it on the radio and the next moment you heard a dance band. You sat eating in restaurants and read casually of men floating for days in dinghies. God, I was hungry. I began to think of food, sickly and ravenously, and then put it out of my mind. You read and heard of these things, and they stopped having meaning. Well, they had meaning for me now. I suddenly realized that what we were doing was a new experience in the world. Until our time no one had ever been on fire in the air. Until our time there had never been so many people to hear of such things and then to forget them again.

I wanted to speak. Where my stomach should have been there was a distended bladder of air. I pressed Allison's head against it. I must have moved sharply, not thinking, and he groaned.

'Ally?' I said. 'Are you all right, Ally?'

He did not answer. Ellis gave him a little more rum and then I held his mouth closed again.

I looked at the stars and went on thinking. The stars were very frosty and brittle and green. One of them grew bright enough to be reflected, broken up, in the black water. Did my wife care? This, I thought, is a nice moment to reason it out. Neither of us had wanted to have children. We hadn't really wanted much at all except a flat, a lot of small social show,

and a good time. Looking back, I felt we were pretty despic-
able. We had really been attracted by a mutual selfishness.
And then we got to hating each other because the selfishness
of one threatened the selfishness of another. A selfishness that
surrenders is unselfishness. Neither of us would surrender. We
were too selfish to have children; we were too selfish to
trouble about obligations. Finally, we were too selfish to want
each other.

All this, it seemed, had happened a long time ago. Life in
the dinghy had gone on a thousand years. I had never had the
use of my hands, and I had never eaten anything but chocolate
and biscuit and rum. Curious that they were luxuries. I had
never sat anywhere except on the edge of that dinghy, with
the sea beating me up and down, the ice cracking on the sides,
and my feet in freezing water. I had never done anything
except hold Allison with my hands and knees. And now I had
held him so long that we seemed frozen together.

Every time we gave Allison the rum that night, I smelled it
for a long time in the air, thick and sweet. Once it ran down
out of his open mouth over my wrists and very slowly, so as
not to disturb him, I raised my wrists and licked it off. My lips
were sore with salt and, because it was not like drinking from
a cup, the rum burnt the cracks in them. I was cold too and
moving my hands was like moving some part of Allison's
body, not my own.

Then once more the rum ran out of Allison's mouth and
poured over my hands, and suddenly I thought it strange that
he could not hold it. I waited for Ellis to crawl back across the
dinghy and sit down. Then I tried to find Allison's hands.
They were loose and heavy at his sides. I tried to move his
head, so that I could speak to him. His face was white in the
starlight. I bent down at last and touched it with my own.

'Ally,' I thought. 'Jesus, Ally. Jesus, Jesus.'

His mouth was stiff and open and his face was colder than the frost could ever make it.

X

I held him for the rest of that night, not telling even Ellis he was dead. It was then about three o'clock. I felt that it was not the frost or the sea or the wind that had killed him. He had been dead for a long time. He had been dead ever since he walked out of the bombed house with the child in his arms.

The death of Allison made me feel very small. Until morning, when the others knew, it did not depress me. For the rest of the night, in the darkness, with the frost terribly vicious in the hours up to seven o'clock, my jacket stiff with ice where the spray had frozen and the ice thin and crackling in the well of the dinghy, I felt it was a personal thing between myself and Allison. I had got myself into the war because, at first, it was an escape from my wife. It was an escape from the wrong way of doing the toast in the morning, the way she spilled powder on her dressing-gown, the silly songs she sang in the bathroom. It was an escape from little things that I magnified by selfishness into big things. I think I wanted to show her, too, that I was capable of some sort of bravery; as if I had any idea what that was.

Now, whatever I had done seemed small beside what Allison had done. I remember how Allison and his wife had wanted the baby, how it had come after Allison had joined up, how its responsibilities excited them. I saw now what he must have felt when he walked out of the bombed house with all his excitement, his joy and his responsibilities compressed into a piece of dead flesh in his hands. I understood why he had been dead a long time.

Just before seven o'clock, when it became light enough for us to see each other, I called Ellis and told him Allison was dead. The thing was a great shock to the rest of us and I saw a look of terror on Ossy's face. Then Ellis and Mac took Allison and laid him, as best they could, in the bottom of the dinghy. None of us felt like saying much and it was Mac who covered Allison's face with his handkerchief, which fluttered and threatened to blow away in the wind.

'It's tough tit, Ally boy. It's tough tit,' he said.

I felt very lonely.

XI

The wind blew away the handkerchief about ten minutes later, leaving the face bare and staring up at us. The handkerchief floated on the sea and floated away fast on bars of foam that were coming up stronger now with the morning wind. We stared for a moment at the disappearing handkerchief, because it was a more living thing than Allison's face lying in the sloppy yellow ice-water in the dinghy, and then Thompson, who never spoke much unless he had something real to say, suggested we should wrap him in his parachute.

'At least we can cover him with it,' he said.

So while Ed and Ossy paddled and Thompson baled what water he could and I sat there helpless, trying to get some flexibility into the arms cramped by holding Allison all night, Mac and Ellis wrapped the body roughly, as best they could, in the parachute. Mac lifted the body in his arms while Ellis and Thompson baled ice and water from the dinghy, and then Ellis spread the parachute. Together they wrapped Allison in it like a mummy.

'Christ, why didn't we think of this before?' Ellis said. 'It would have kept him warm. I blame myself.'

'He died a long time ago,' I said.

'He what?'

'You couldn't have done anything,' I said.

Soon they finished wrapping him in the parachute and he seemed to cover almost all the space in the dinghy, so that we had nowhere to put our feet and we kept pushing them against him. The sun was up now, pale yellow in a flat sky, but it was still freezing. The sea seemed to be going past at a tremendous pace, black and white and rough, as if we were travelling with a current or a tide.

I could see that Ossy and Ed Walker were terribly dejected. We were all pale and tired, with bluish dark eyes, and stubby beards which seemed to have sucked all the flesh from our cheek-bones. But Ossy and Ed, partly through the intense cold, much more through the shock of Allison's death, seemed to have sunk into that vacant and silent state in which Allison himself had been on the previous afternoon. They were staring flatly at the sea.

'O.K., chaps,' Ellis said, 'breakfast now.'

He began to ration out the biscuits and the chocolate. One piece of chocolate had a piece of white paper round it. As Ellis unwrapped it the wind tore it overboard. It too, like the handkerchief, went away at great speed, as if we were travelling on a tide.

Suddenly Ellis stopped in the act of holding a piece of chocolate to my mouth. I opened my mouth ready to bite it. So we both sat transfixed, I with my mouth open, Ellis holding the chocolate about three inches away.

'You see it?' he said. 'You see it? You see?'

'Looks like a floating elephant,' Mac said.

'It's a buoy!' Ellis said. 'Don't you see, it's a buoy!'

'Holy Moses,' Mac said.

'Paddle!' Ellis said. 'For Christ's sake, paddle! All of you, paddle.'

I made a violent grab at the chocolate with my mouth, partly biting it and Ellis's finger before it was snatched away. Ellis swore and we all laughed like hell. The sight of that buoy, rocking about half a mile westwards, like drunken elephant, encouraged us into a light-hearted frenzy, in which at intervals we laughed again for no reason at all.

'We're going in with the tide,' I said. 'I've been watching it.'

'Paddle like hell!' Ellis said. 'Straight for the buoy. Paddle!'

I paddled with my mind. They said afterwards that I paddled also with my hands. The buoy seemed to go past us, two or three minutes later, at a devil of a speed, though it was we who were travelling. The wind had freshened with the sun and we seemed to bounce on the waves, shipping water. But we had forgotten about baling now. We had forgotten almost about the body of Allison, rolling slightly in the white parachute in the dirty sea-water at our feet. We had forgotten about everything except frantically paddling with the tide.

It was likely that we should have seen land a long time before this, except that it was without cliffs and was a low line of sand unlit by sun. In the far distance there was a slight haze which turned to blue and amber as the sun rose. Then across the mist and the colour the line of land broke like a long wave of brown.

Ten minutes later there was hardly any need to paddle at all. The tide was taking us in fast, in a calmer stretch of water, towards a flat, wide beach of sand. Beyond it there was no town. There were only telegraph wires stretching up and down the empty coast, and soon we were so near that I could see where the snow had beaten and frozen on the black poles, in white stripes on the seaward side.

I looked at my watch as we floated in, not paddling now, on the tide. It was about eight o'clock and we had been, as far as I could tell, nearly sixty hours in the dinghy.

Then as we came in, and the exhilaration of beating in towards the coast on that fast tide began to lessen, I became aware of things. I became aware of my hands. They were swollen from lack of attention and stiff from holding Allison. I became aware of hunger. The hollowness of my stomach filled at intervals with the sickness of hunger and then emptied again. I became aware again of Allison, wrapped in the parachute, once very white, now dirty with sea-water and the excited marks of our feet, and I became aware, in one clear moment before the dinghy struck the sand, of Ellis and Mac and Ed and Thompson and all that they now meant to me. I became aware of Ossy, standing in the dinghy like a crazy person, waving his spanner.

When the dinghy hit the sand and would go no further I jumped overboard. There was no feeling of impact as my legs struck the shore. They seemed hollow and dead. They folded under me as if made of straw and I fell on my face on the wet sand of the beach, helpless, and lay there like a fool.

And as I lay there, the sand wet and cold and yet good on my face, I became aware of a final thing. We had been out a long way, and through a great deal together. We had been through fire and water, death and frost, and had come home.

And soon we should go out again.

THE BEGINNING OF THINGS

THE SUDDEN ARRIVAL of Me. 109's over the island in these early days was not pleasant. Even when they ran away they were good. They were very fast and after the Macchis they seemed very formidable and in the evenings there used to be long discussions in the Squadron on how to get them down.

McAlister was then about twenty: one of those people who are learning elementary physics one day, while a war is being planned by older men, who are wearing medals the next, by which time older men are already discussing what should happen when the war is over. The war was not over for McAlister by any means. The war and his life were the same thing: he did not want either to end. A D.F.C. and bar and four Macchis and six dive-bombers down were only part of life: a few strips torn off, a wizard time, the beginning of things. He had been very scared most of the time, and at the same time very eager, very tense and very excited. He had a nice word for being scared, but it is not printable either. Unfortunately I do not know what he thought of the men who made it, but no doubt that is unprintable too.

The spring weather was already hot on Malta when the first Me.'s began to appear. The young wheat was high and green in the fields and the sea very blue on the hot afternoons beyond the harbour. It was cool at night and on the nine o'clock watch in the mornings.

One morning the Hurricanes scrambled shortly after nine. Soon they were over Luca at twenty thousand. Far over Luca they were still climbing when the first Me.'s swooped down on them out of the sun. They swooped down very fast, screaming, and the Hurricanes split apart into a circle. This was as they had planned and McAlister took his place in the circle and looked about him. Just then the second Me.'s came down out of the sun, screaming like the first, trying to break the segment of the circle where McAlister was.

It all happened very quickly. McAlister turned back under the Me.'s and they overshot him. He looked round and there was nothing to see. And then he turned back and there in front of him was the Me. he wanted. It was the Me. he had wanted for a long time, the one they had all wanted. He felt that if he could shoot it down it would be more than a personal triumph. It would be perhaps even more than a Squadron triumph. It would be the first Me. shot down over the island and it would be a victory for morale. He wanted it very badly. His hands were shaking and his blood was thumping very heavily in his throat and his mouth was sour as it watered. He was closing in very fast and he felt that nothing could stop him now.

The moment the crash came in his own cockpit he knew what an awful fool he had been. He had been much too excited to look in the mirror. And now he had made that utterly foolish, perhaps utterly fatal mistake. The cockpit was full of flying metal and the spray of blood. He went at once into a steep spiral dive. He was very angry with himself: very, very angry that he had been such a fool, that he had been beaten so easily, for the first time, at his own game.

When he came out of the dive he saw that his left arm was

dripping with blood and when he tried to lift it it would not move. He did not know quite what else was happening. He afterwards remembered standing up in the cockpit. He remembered quite clearly, before that, how he opened the hood and disconnected his oxygen. He remembered breaking the R/T connexions too. But between the moment of standing up and the moment of seeing his kite dive away from him and of hearing the fading roar of the engine as it fell to earth he did not remember anything at all. He remembered nothing of being angry any longer, or scared, or even in pain.

He knew only that it was a wonderful feeling to be out of the kite, in the air, quite free and at least temporarily safe, in the enormous peaceful space of sky. He could hear nothing except the dying roar of his kite going down to earth and once, above it, a long burst of cannon fire. He knew quite well, and quite intelligently, that he was upside down. It was a little ridiculous; his legs cut off his upward view. His arm was beginning suddenly to pain him very much and because of this he decided to pull the cord. He had been very stuck by the notion that he might faint and never pull it at all.

When he went to pull the cord it was not there. For a moment it seemed to him that the chute must have been torn away from him as he left the kite. He was falling upside down and this was the end. He afterwards remembered thinking how very simple it was. You were shot down and you fell upside down and you found there was no chute and really, after all, it was simpler, less painful, less horrible business than you had always imagined dying to be. You would fall a very long way and would hit the deck with a very hard thud, but the impact and pain would by that time no longer matter. Your arm would cease hurting for ever and nobody would ever attack you behind again. At home your parents would read the telegram about your death and perhaps there would be a notice of it in *The Times*. Your mother would cry and the real pain of loss and emptiness and sacrifice and despair would not be yours, but theirs, and it would be far away and you would never know.

And finally, thinking this, he made one last effort to see if his parachute was with him. He snatched for the cord and suddenly it was there. He held it in his hands. He pulled it violently, and suddenly it was as if he were being hanged. The upward force of the chute opening seemed to wrench the upper part of his body away from the rest. The harness tightened with great power. He could not breathe and he felt very ill. Waves of darkness began to float over him and blood flashed back into his face, in windy spurts, from the wounded arm. The pain of the arm was savage and the pain of not being able to breathe, stupefying him, was worse. He saw Malta far below him, like a misty map in the sun, and all he wanted now was to be there, to lie on this map like the inanimate mark of a town, peacefully, without movement and without pain.

He must have gone off at this moment into a stupor, perhaps a faint, brought on by pain and shock and the loss of blood. He came out of it to hear the noise of an aircraft. It seemed to be bearing down on him and he had a notion at that moment, once again, that all was over. He was going to be holed like a bloody colander by an Me. who had followed him down. This, and nothing else, was the experience of being shot down. This was the killing part. You were hung up like a half-dead pheasant on a string and an Me. who had nothing else to do came down and did circles round you at leisure and fired until your guts ran out like jelly.

He looked up at last and saw not an Me. but a Hurricane. 'Thank Christ,' he thought. 'Oh! thank Christ for that.'

The Hurricane circled a few times but he was too tired, too weak, and still too much in pain to show his joy. He was holding the raw stump of the wounded arm with his other arm and he could not wave his hands. He shut his eyes and drifted away, swinging, as if he were drunk and the world were spinning round.

When he opened his eyes again the Hurricane had gone and he could see the town more clearly. But it was still far down and once or twice he swung very violently and because of his hands he could not stop the swinging. He felt very sick and then finally he fell faster, not caring much until he looked down and felt that the roofs of the town, hot in the sun, were flying upward like enormous missiles that would hit him and lift him skyward again. Then for a time he drifted away, more to the edge of the town, and soon it was only the flat roof of a little house that was rushing up to meet him. There was the little house and beside it was a little patch of wheat. The wheat was very green and McAlister saw it wave and shimmer in the wind and sun.

He hit the ground with great violence and rolled over. He lay still and this, at last, he thought, is the moment. I have been falling twenty-five thousand feet for the privilege of this moment, for the sweetness, the calm, the painlessness and the silence of being able to die. There is nothing else now. The chute does not matter, nor the arm, nor the pain. It is enough to lie in the wheat and shut my eyes against the sun and wait for the moment, and myself, to end.

The crowd of gesticulating Maltese who rushed up to him, trampling the wheat and tearing off his chute and holding up his head, made him very furious. They stopped all his thoughts about dying. He was not going to be bumped about like a piece of beef by anybody and he let out with extraordinary strength with his feet. It was as if the Maltese wanted to tear him to pieces for souvenirs. He kicked very hard for a few moments, just to show how very living he was, and then his strength slipped out of him and he lay emptily on the earth, too tired to be angry again, only telling the Maltese how to give him morphia and how to bind the tourniquet.

A little later they carried him across the little field of wheat to the advanced dressing station, and then to the town. He did not know much what happened. Two days later they took off his arm and in the night he was very restless and used to amuse himself sometimes scaring the Sister by telling her he would die because he did not want her to go away. The arm did not smell very nice in the days before they took it off and he was terrified that, without the arm, he would never fly again. But in fifteen days, from that moment, he was flying solo.

He is flying solo still. He flies beautifully and dangerously and they have fitted him up with an arm that has many intricate devices. You can see the delight of being able to fly in his face. It is one of the faces of those who fight wars they do not make and for whom flying and life are one: the faces of those who should be watched, the faces of the young – not of the young who die, but of the young who are shot down and live – of the young who are at the beginning of things.

THE DISINHERITED

ON THAT STATION we had pilots from all over the world, so that the sound of the mess, as someone said, was like a Russian bazaar. They came from Holland and Poland, Belgium and Czechoslovakia, France and Norway. We had many French and they had with them brown and yellow men from the Colonial Empire who at dispersal on warm spring afternoons played strange games with pennies in the dry, white dust on the edge of the perimeter. We had many Canadians and New Zealanders, Australians and Africans. There was a West Indian boy, the colour of milky coffee, who was a barrister, and a Lithuanian who played international football. There was a man from Indo-China and another from Tahiti. There was an American and a Swiss and there were negroes, very black and curly, among the ground-crews. We had men who had done everything and been everywhere, who had had everything and had lost it all. They had escaped across frontiers and over mountains and down the river valleys of Central Europe; they had come through Libya and Iran and Turkey and round the Cape; they had come through Spain and Portugal or nailed under the planks of little ships wherever a little ship could put safely to sea. They had things in common with themselves that men had nowhere else on earth, and you saw on their faces sometimes a look of sombre silence that could only have been the expression of recollected hatred. But among them all there was only one who had something which no one else had, and he was Capek the Czech. Capek had white hair.

Capek was a night fighter pilot, so that mostly in the daytime you would find him in the hut at dispersal. The hut was very pleasant and there was a walnut piano and a radio and a miniature billiard table and easy chairs that had been presented by the mayor of the local town. No one ever played the piano but it was charming all the same. On the walls there were pictures, some in colour, of girls in their underwear and without underwear at all, and rude remarks about pilots who forgot to check their guns. Pilots who had been flying at night lay on the camp beds, sleeping a little, their eyes puffed, using their flying jackets as pillows; or they played cards and groused and talked shop among themselves. They were bored because they were flying too much. They argued about the merits of a four-cannon job as opposed to those of a single gun that fires through the airscrew. They argued about the climate of New Zealand, if it could be compared with the climate of England. They were restless and temperamental, as fighter pilots are apt to be, and it seemed always as if they would have been happier doing anything but the things they were.

Capek alone did not do these things. He did not seem bored or irritable, or tired or temperamental. He did not play billiards and he did not seem interested in the bodies of the girls on the walls. He was never asleep on the beds. He never played cards or argued about the merits of this or that. It seemed sometimes as if he did not belong to us. He sat apart from us, and with his white hair, cultured brown face, clean fine lips and the dark spectacles he wore sometimes against the bright spring sunlight he looked something like a middle-aged provincial professor who had come to take a cure at a health resort in the sun. Seeing him in the street, the bus, the train or the tram, you would never have guessed that he could fly. You would never have guessed that in order to be one of us, to fly with us and fight with us, Capek had come half across the world.

There was a time when a very distinguished personage came to the station and, seeing Capek, asked how long he had been in the Air Force and Capek replied 'Please, seventeen years.' This took his flying life far back beyond the beginning of the war we were fighting; back to the years when some of us were hardly born and when Czechoslovakia had become born again as a nation. Capek had remained in the Air Force all those years, flying heaven knows what types of 'plane, and becoming finally part of the forces that crumbled away and disintegrated and disappeared under the progress of the tanks that entered Prague in the summer of 1939. Against this progress Capek was one of those who disappeared. He disappeared in a lorry with many others and they rode eastward towards Poland, always retreating and not knowing where they were going. With Capek was a man named Machakek, and as the retreat went on Capek and Machakek became friends.

Capek and Machakek stayed in Poland all that summer, until the chaos of September. It is not easy to know what Capek and Machakek did; if they were interned, or how, or where, because Capek's English is composed of small difficult words and long difficult silences, often broken only by smiles. 'All time is retreat. Then war start. Poland is in war. Then Germany is coming one way and Russia is coming another.' In this way Capek and Machakek had no escape. They could go neither east nor west. It was too late to go south, and in the north Gdynia had gone. And in time, as Germany moved eastward and Russia westward, Capek and Machakek were taken by the Russians. Capek went to a concentration camp, and Machakek worked in the mines. As prisoners they had a status not easy to define. Russia was not then in the war and Czechoslovakia, politically, did not exist. It seemed in these days as if Russia might come into the war against us. It was very confused and during the period of clarification, if you could call it that, Capek and Machakek went on working in the concentration camp and the mine. 'We remain,' Capek said, 'one year and three-quarter.'

Then the war clarified and finally Capek was out of the concentration camp and Machakek was out of the mine. They were together again, still friends, and they moved south, to the Black Sea. Standing on the perimeter track, in the bright spring sun, wearing his dark spectacles, Capek had so little to say about this that he looked exactly like a blind man who has arrived somewhere, after a long time, but for whom the journey is darkness. 'From Black Sea I go to Turkey. Turkey then to Syria. Then Cairo. Then Aden.'

'And Machakek with you?'

'Machakek with me, yes. But only to Aden. After Aden Machakek is going to Bombay on one boat. I am going to Cape Town on other.'

'So Machakek went to India?'

'To India, yes. Is very long way. Is very long time.'

'And you – Cape Town?'

'Yes, me, Cape Town. Then Gibraltar. Then here, England.'

'And Machakek?'

'Machakek is here too. We are both post here. To this squadron.'

The silence that followed this had nothing to do with the past; it had much to do with the present; more to do with

Machakek. Through the retreat and the mine and the concentration camp, through the journey to Turkey and Cairo and Aden, through the long sea journey to India and Africa, and finally England, Capek and Machakek had been friends. When a man speaks only the small words of a language that is not his own he finds it hard to express the half-tones of hardship and relief and suffering and most of what Capek and Machakek had suffered together was in Capek's white hair. But now something had happened which was not expressed there but which lay in the dark, wild eyes behind the glasses and the long silences of Capek as he sat staring at the Hurricanes in the sun. His friend Machakek was dead.

The handling of night fighters is not easy. It was perhaps hard for Capek and Machakek that they should come out of the darkness of Czechoslovakia, through the darkness of the concentration camp and the mine, in order to fight in darkness. It was hard for Machakek who, overshooting the drome, hit a telegraph post and died before Capek could get there. It was harder still for Capek, who was now alone.

But the hardest part of it all, perhaps, is that Capek cannot talk to us. He does not know words that will express what he feels about the end of Machakek's journey. He does not know words like endurance and determination, imperishable and undefeated, sacrifice, and honour. They are the words, anyway, that are never mentioned at dispersals. He does not know the words for grief and friendship, home-sickness and loss. They are never mentioned at dispersals either. Above all he does not know the words for himself and what he has done.

I do not know the words for Capek either. Looking at his white hair, his dark eyes and his long hands, I am silent now.

CROIX DE GUERRE

IT WAS RATHER difficult to imagine what sort of man he had been in France, in the days before the War, because even with the uniform of the French pilot he did not look very French. He looked more than anything else like an English publican: large, stolid, bright-eyed, with very red cheeks flushed raw with blue. You might otherwise perhaps have thought of him as a taxi-driver in Boulogne, which is where he came from, sitting half the day in the sun on the running-board of the taxi while waiting for the boats to come in and now and then going heavily across the street, cap on the back of his head, for a drink or two in the shade of the café. He looked less French than any Frenchman in the Squadron and more English, perhaps, than any Englishman. The only very French thing about him was a slight pout of the lips and a shrug of the shoulders as he used his favourite expression – 'C'est tout' – by which he always minimized any achievement that you thought remarkable. He said what he had to say in the heavy and formal manner of an English police sergeant giving evidence straight from the notebook at the local petty sessions. He was the sort of man who did not stop to describe the view. What he had done was, according to him, very straightforward, very simple, very dull and he gave the impression, entirely without fuss, that there might even have been a mistake about the Croix de Guerre.

He had, in fact, been a civilian pilot before the war, operating, I daresay, on one of the French internal airways. He had all the calm tenacity of temperament that makes the good bomber pilot and from his description of life in the early part of the war, if you could call his flat statement of facts a description, you got a picture of a routine that was duller than the driving of English tourists from the docks at Boulogne to the cathedral in a taxi on hot summer afternoons. You could picture the French pilots, though he did not describe it, playing *banque* in the crew rooms of the dispersal hut, and the ground-crews playing strange games with *sous* in the dust outside. You could picture them off duty, rather swagger in their dark-blue uniforms with much gold braid, as they sauntered on spring evenings in the local town, wondering perhaps not of what kind of war it was and if it would ever end, but also if it would ever begin.

When it did begin, with shocking suddenness, in the May of 1940, Poirot was almost immediately shot down and the end of things was already very near. But three or four days of the life of France still remained when he got back to his unit near Boulogne – just long enough for him to discover that there were no longer any 'planes, that there would be no 'planes and that all he could do now was to see that his men were armed and that they understood the state of things and were ready. There was no swaggering in blue and gold uniforms in the evening sunlight now. Poirot and his men moved into Le Touquet. They were no longer part of the French Air Force. Having no 'planes they were, sooner perhaps than most Frenchmen, disinherited. The British were leaving, but Poirot and his men had no orders to leave and when the time at last became very short, they dug themselves into the casino.

I do not know how long they remained there: three or four days perhaps; at any rate until things became hopeless. They were – I gathered it more from the expression on Poirot's face than from anything he said – very tenacious. As it became hopeless a few of them slipped out under cover of darkness. The rest, with Poirot, remained, and they remained there until there was nothing to do but surrender, or be captured, whichever way it was.

'They began to march us back to Germany,' Poirot said, as if it were no more than a walk along the coast from Le Touquet. The weather was very beautiful in the early summer of that year and the nights were starry and dark and fine and I could imagine Poirot being driven eastward along the hot roads like one of a string of cattle, his red, solid bovine face giving no sort of hint of the man he was. The second night – or it might have been the third or fourth night, at least while they were still in France – Poirot escaped. If the impression is that he turned round and walked back, as if the walk beyond Le Touquet had begun to bore him, the impression is as good as any other. In two days he was back in Boulogne. It was full of Nazis now and the war, for all that mattered, was over.

For three weeks Poirot hid there with friends. They may have been bakers or taxi-drivers, or café proprietors or grocers, or officials from the port. Poirot, for very good reasons, does not give the artistic details. Supposing they were bakers, it became necessary in time to move to the café. It had become very dangerous. But in time, as June came on, it began to seem safer. Poirot then got hold of a bicycle and began to ride south, and I seem to see him, very hot, very red, very tenacious, pounding along the straight French roads between the pillars of poplar leaves in the bright June nights like a competitor in one of those non-stop national bicycle races of which the French are so fond. He must have ridden for a long time, sleeping by day, riding by night, until he came to within reach of the unoccupied zone. There all the bridges over the Loire were guarded and so Poirot left the bicycle and swam the river, and once again I seem to see him, huge, red, tenacious, pounding now at the water with his sun-brown arms in immense determination. Swimming across the river, bicycling down the roads, walking back to Le Touquet, hiding in the casino, Poirot all the time seems to exhibit qualities for which we give the French no credit. He moves along to predetermined places like an ox. 'C'est tout,' he says, as if he had no imagination at all.

At Toulon, which he evidently reached in the July of that year, Poirot demanded to be demobilized. It was his right. But the authorities, who seemed to have had more than a suspicion of the qualities that lay behind that extremely stolid and phlegmatic face, thought quite otherwise. They were very much in need of men like Poirot. 'We need you in North Africa,' they said. It may have been this action of theirs that upset Poirot. He may have reasoned that escaping from Nazis, defending casinos, hiding in houses, bicycling across France and swimming rivers, deserved a slight reward. The reward that Poirot wanted was quite simple. He wanted freedom. Unfortunately the authorities at Toulon had none of it to give away.

But instead, they said in Africa, we will give you the Croix de Guerre. I do not know what kind of medal the Croix de Guerre is. Possibly it is a very nice medal. Possibly Poirot was very honoured to have it. He does not say. He does not fill in the emotional details of the story. But it seemed to me that he acted with a curious kind of sardonic frivolity for a man who is pleased to be decorated.

What is quite evident is that Poirot had decided that he did not like the Vichy authorities at all. The day when the medals were to be presented to Poirot and his comrades was, as I imagine it always is with the French, a very ceremonial affair. Poirot, who looks so unimaginative and who does not bother with details, did not describe the scene, but it is not hard to see the Glen Martins lined up about the track in the African sun, the blue and braid of the pilots' uniforms as they wait at attention, the glitter of the big-wigs, the ceremonial kisses of presentation. Poirot does not describe, either, his emotions at this scene. But they, too, were probably very direct and very clear. For Poirot was probably the most nervous man of all.

After the presentation of medals the squadrons flew over the drome, giving one of those serene and ordered displays which are part of the ceremonial. Thinking of their flying over the drome, I like to think also of those who were watching below: the high officials, the caps of gold braid, the rows of medals, the distinguished uplifted faces watching the circling planes. Poirot does not fill in these details, for the simple reason that he was too high and too occupied to notice them. I like to think very much of the serene solemnity of the official faces, of Poirot flying above them, rather like a rude Donald Duck who does not know his ceremonial manners. I like above all to imagine their faces, their French volubility, their indignant dignity and their final horror as Poirot at last turned his plane away, helped by a navigator and a radio operator who valued freedom, and set his course for Gibraltar.

I like too the way in which Poirot ends his story, phlegmatically, briefly, unexcitedly, as you would expect him to end it. 'C'est tout,' he says.

YOURS IS THE EARTH

HE USED TO fly one of the morning mails to the Continent before the war: a steady and at the same time a shaky job, done in all sorts of weather, that finally built for him a total of three thousand hours. He must have known the way across the Channel as a man knows the way, in light or darkness, up his own garden path. As pilots go he was really quite old too: over thirty, really quite old. He had a wife and family too and when the Nazis killed them in a blitz there was no longer anything to be done with him. He became one of those legendary figures that read alone in their rooms and fret to be flying and curse the controller and the weather: one of those who ask only to be free for revenge, who are slightly insane in their desire to equal the score and who are talked about in messes long after they are dead.

They are the sort of individualists – sometimes exiles, sometimes men with lost limbs – whom you seem to find always among the night fighters. They are those who, because they have lost countries or limbs or families or perhaps hope, do not want very much to be disciplined. The war for them has become very personal. For them night is more free than day: free darkness, free stars, free moon, free space for the expression of a feud. They find raiders in the moon above low cloud, shadows in the flare of ack-ack and above the glare of ground fires. They are the intruders who look for Christmas trees: the dromes with their landing light burning and the red and green and yellow eyes of returning planes.

It is often the quietest who hate most, and his reticence was very typical. It really concealed a great ferocity. But when he knocked down eight raiders in one night, he gave all the decorations to the Hurricane. 'She'll fly through anything,' he said, not then really knowing how true it was.

He did not really know that until one night in the early summer of 1941. That night he chased a Heinkel over France and then stalked it, coming very close. Often it is possible to get a Heinkel with a one-second burst; but though he was very close he pressed the button a little longer. The explosion in the Heinkel was immense. It seemed to lift him out of the sky. He seemed to be projected violently upwards and then fall through the vacuum created by the explosion down on to a table of flame. He seemed to skid along this surface of flame, seeing it gradually break and rise until it grew into walls of fire about him. This fire, after a few seconds, blinded him, so that for a long time afterwards his sight was partially blacked out, his night vision gone. He had only the most confused and painful impression of flying through the flames and out of it and beyond it, upside down.

It was all very fantastic. He flew on for what seemed a long time, practically blind. When his night vision came back at last he saw oil spurting and streaming all over the cockpit. He knew that he had to get down. He was a very long way from home and his only hope was a strange aerodrome. He did not know the approaches, but somehow he got down at last, still confused and blinded by that fantastic, inverted projection along a table of flame.

The quiet nights of the summer seemed fantastic in an opposite way after that. He did not like the nights of inactivity. He was always restless, hating and cursing the weather, the long periods of non-operational calm. He must have felt that it needed many nights, many moons, many lights shaken from the Christmas trees before he could come to within a remote distance of making his revenge complete, even if it could be made complete. He had seen his family deprived of the earth and he must have felt that any night when he did not fly was a whole night of wasted opportunity. It was for this impatient anxiety that there was no discipline. To fly, to kill, to smash the pretty lights on the most sinister of all Christmas trees: for God's sake, what had the weather to do with that? Hadn't he flown the mail in all sorts of weather? If you could risk your life to fly to safety the trivial correspondence of peace-time just because somebody was impatient for an answer then you could fly through hell because you yourself were impatient for an answer that could be given only by you and only in one way.

He went on in this fretful and furious way all summer. 'Oh! Yes, he was quite mad,' they say of him now. 'Quite mad. You couldn't tell him what not to do, or if you did he wouldn't do it. He would go off on his own and you couldn't stop him.' He was quite mad and he had reason to be. They had already decorated him handsomely; now they decorated him again. But what he needed, all that summer, was not decoration but simply the chance to fly, to kill and blow out a few more lights in the darkness across the water.

The chance did not come until the end of the summer. He was out on the sea beyond the Norfolk coast and they say he actually screamed at the sight of a Heinkel. It was the scream of a man who does not find it possible, even by time and bloodshed, to neutralize a hatred. It was the scream of a whole summer of released fury and boredom and inactivity.

He drove the Heinkel inexorably down to sea-level. As it jettisoned its bombs, which threw up huge columns of water, he rose away from these water spouts and then when they cleared at last closed in again and opened fire. The moment when the Heinkel struck the sea in clouds of smoke and steam was the moment for which he had waited. It did something to set him free.

They decorated him again for that. And then, as always, when fighters become very expert, very successful and very intent on bloody results, they gave him a special mission.

He went off to do it in the calm twilight of an autumn evening. The time between departure and return, for a Hurricane, is not long. The time went by and the short margin of time behind it went by too until it became clear that the anger, the hatred and the desire for revenge had been dissipated at last.

He is the dead now – you are the living. His was the sky – yours is the earth because of him.

THERE'S SOMETHING IN THE AIR

ALL THAT SPRING and summer we lived in a big, old cream house surrounded by trees that lay under the downs within sight of the sea. The walls of the mess were bright green, but it was never a green like the green of the fresh-mown lawns of the house, or the new leaves of the limes, or the green of the summer meadows under the hills. On hot clear days the sea-light over the sea made the high clouds like ripples of snow and the barrage balloons of passing ships melted into the sky like big bubbles of shining cloud.

Neither Anderson nor Auerbach got up till twelve. Because they were night fighters their night was day, and part of their day was night, and in this and a few other simple facts they were alike, doing the same things. The few simple facts were that they flew Hurricanes, belonged to the same squadron, were very volatile and had shot down many aircraft by night. But in everything else it seemed to me they had nothing in common at all.

Anderson was English; Auerbach was Czech. Anderson was about six foot two, but Auerbach was a little man about five feet and a half. Anderson had gone practically straight from school to fly, but Auerbach had first to escape from Czechoslovakia down into the Mediterranean and through North Africa and so to France before he was able to reach

England. Anderson, fair and fresh-faced, with a small corn-brown moustache, looked rather aristocratic in a manner that could not have been anything else but British. His moustache alone was an emblem, plain as the Union Jack.

But Auerbach did not look particularly Czech or, though his ancestors had been notable military people, particularly aristocratic. He did not look particularly anything. He had in him something of the element of the anonymous peasant. In his tender, crafty, smiling blue eyes there was a profound watchfulness. It was the sort of look that might have been inherited from generations of people perpetually wondering how long the things they possess are going to remain their own. They are watching to see that they are not cheated. That look sometimes made Auerbach, in spite of a sort of a cunning vivacity, look quite old.

In many other things Anderson and Auerbach were not the same. Anderson was very much the young blood whose life was split fairly evenly between flying and girls, and his free week-ends were beautiful and wild. Auerbach had married an English girl, and was now a settled man. He sometimes looked rather shy and there was a record of how once, before he was married, he had taken a girl out for the evening and how, in the darkness, coming home, he had kissed her good night on the forehead.

All that late spring and early summer Anderson and Auerbach flew together. It was one of those periods in a station when the unity and life of a good squadron becomes too strong to become a local thing, compressed within itself, meaning something only to a few people. It breaks out, and spreading, warm and energetic and fluid, becomes a large thing, meaning something to many people.

It was one of those periods when everything was good. The weather was good and calm and sunny, the sea-light lofty and pure over the sea by day. The nights were good and starry, with no ground mist and just the right cover of cloud. The squadron was good and proud and knew itself. The things it did were good and the news of its doings was in the papers. Whenever you came into the mess of the billiard-room or the dining-room and heard laughter boiling over too richly you knew it was that squadron laughing. You knew by their laughter that they wanted nothing else than to be kept as they were, flying by night together, shooting up trains on the flat lands of Northern France, shooting down careless Dorniers over their own aerodromes. They had found each other. The positive and exuberant feeling of their discovery spread over the station, from Erks to Waafs and from Waafs to officers, until all of us felt it there.

But the best of all that feeling came from Anderson and Auerbach. Every night Anderson and Auerbach flew out over Northern France, separately, to wait for enemy bombers coming home from raids on Britain. And every morning, when we came down to breakfast, long before Anderson and Auerbach were up, we heard only one question. It was not 'What is there for breakfast?' or 'What is in the papers?' as if we had any fond ideas that either would be any different from the morning before, but only 'How many did Anderson and Auerbach shoot down?'

When that spring began Anderson and Auerbach had each shot down nine aircraft, all by day. The weather in the winter had been very bad. The long period of inaction began to be broken in the month of April. It had then been a long time since either Anderson or Auerbach had shot anything down. Now they began to shoot something down almost every night. It struck me that what they were doing was very like poaching: something of the same instinct took them alone, across Channel, to roam craftily above the dromes of Northern

France, waiting for stray victims. It was only in the way they did this that they seemed, as always and in almost everything else, very different. Anderson's way was to choose an aero-drome and fly to it and impatiently round it, waiting for the drome lights to be switched on and watching for the navi-gation light of returning bombers. If the light did not come on very soon he lost eagerness and flew away to another drome, always impatient and volatile and eager until something hap-pened, always furious and blasphemous when nothing did.

But all that Auerbach did was to wait. Auerbach had patience. It was the patience of craftiness: of the man who sits above a rabbit hole, waiting to strike. Auerbach had come from Czechoslovakia and the Mediterranean and North Africa and France for the purpose of striking and now, as I looked at it, a few moments' more waiting would not matter. So it was Anderson, they said, who had the brilliance and Auerbach, they said, who had the luck: whereas it was really only the difference between a man who had infinite patience and one who had none at all.

So almost every morning, by one or two and sometimes three aircraft, we heard that Anderson and Auerbach had raised the score; and almost every noon I used to see Anderson and Auerbach themselves, getting up after their late sleep. What they told me and the way they told it was, as always, very different.

About noon Auerbach was always in the billiard-room. He was not particularly good but he played like a clown in a circus and there was always a crowd watching him. He had a droll and magnetic way of laughing and the laughter in the billiard-room used to bubble over when Auerbach was there.

'Nice going,' I would say. 'What were they?'

'I think all Dornier 217's. I'm not sure. Perhaps one Heinkel 111.'

'Very nice.'

'Peez of cake.'

Every noon, while Auerbach was playing billiards, Anderson was on the terrace of the house, sun-bathing, alone. Auerbach used to say very little. He used to give a wink and a nod and a flick of his thumb and it was an understanding between us: the common language that needed no elaboration. But Anderson, lying back on the cream stone terrace, eyes shaded against the sun, his moustache looking more corn-brown and more British than ever against his naked body, liked to talk about what happened. 'Yes, and Auerbach got three! Two Dorniers and a Heinkel and a probable, the sod. God, he has the luck. There I stayed over the same drome for twenty minutes and not a sausage. Five minutes after I leave it Auerbach comes and they light up the whole bloody Christmas tree.'

'Luck,' I said.

'Luck, hell,' he said. 'He's got some sixth sense or something. He knows which bloody drome they'll use and when they'll use it.'

'Just crafty,' I said. 'You can see it in his eyes.'

'Crafty as hell,' he said.

'And you?' I said. 'I hear you got one?'

'One solitary 217. They switched all the bloody drome lights on and there they were, as big as hell, about a dozen of them. Then as soon as I hit them they put everything out and I was finished.'

'You must be equal with Auerbach now,' I said.

'No he's one up on me. The lucky sod, he's always one up on me.'

'Tomorrow you'll probably get six,' I said.

'Me?' he said. 'The only time I ever see six is when the bloody ammo. runs out.'

What he said turned out to be true. The next night he saw twenty; the lights of the drome and the lights of the bombers were like the lights of a party round a Christmas tree. Anderson went in with great excitement and began to line them up. He hit the first Dornier at only a hundred feet, and she blew up underneath him almost before he had time to pull out of the dive. There is something about being hit at a hundred feet which does not seem to be in the rules and the confusion must have been very great.

The lights of the drome continued to burn as brilliantly as ever and the lights of the incoming bombers were not switched off. All Anderson had to do was to turn and come in again and hit a Heinkel. He saw it crash in wreaths of orange fire in the black space beyond the circle of light. Then he hit another and he saw it too burning among the lights, as if something in the Christmas tree had fallen and caught fire. Even then the lights of the drome still kept burning and the bombers circled round like coloured fire-flies. It was all so fantastic, with the red and white light shining in the darkness and the coloured lights moving in the sky and the orange fires breaking the darkness, that Anderson could not believe it to be true. It was only when he had the fourth bomber lined up and pressed the tit and nothing happened except a fraction of a second burst that he knew the ammo. was spent and it was real after all.

I do not know how many Auerbach got that night; but by the end of May he and Anderson were still almost equal, and by the beginning of June what they did was in the papers every day. The papers had their photographs too and I suppose the photographs were something like them. But what the papers printed was really a comic story. It was the story of two men with eagle eyes, though sometimes it was cat's eyes and sometimes it was hawk's eyes, who stalked over France every night in the darkness.

We liked especially the word stalk, since it is the one thing an aeroplane does not do, and thinking of the clear, youthful, exuberant eyes of Anderson and of the crafty, friendly blue eyes of Auerbach, we liked the nonsense about the eyes. From the newspapers you got the impression that Anderson and Auerbach were a pair of heroic bandits who behaved with copybook courage and were in some way supernatural. This attitude was perhaps excusable, since the newspapers never saw Anderson lying naked in the sun, blaspheming about the luck of Auerbach, or Auerbach playing snooker, with a laughing audience who got more fun out of Auerbach potting the black than they got out of his putting a Heinkel down.

It was excusable because, after all, the newspapers could not know the feeling that comes from a squadron which is at the crest of things: the warm and positive excitement that we felt all that spring and which went on expanding and flowing outward all that summer. They did not know about Auerbach playing billiards and comic games of snooker, or about his kissing a girl on the forehead in the dark. They did not know about Anderson lying on his back in the sun and looking at the green summer leaves and the green grass spreading to the foot of the dark hills and saying, a little solemnly, because this was his first year in England since the war began: 'You can't believe how bloody wizard it is. You can't know what it is to see the leaves so green on the trees.'

There seemed no reason why this feeling and this squadron, and above all why Anderson and Auerbach, should not have gone on for ever. There seemed no reason why Anderson and Auerbach should ever stop those simple and disastrous journeys over France. But there comes a time when every squadron is held to have earned its rest; when some obscure department somewhere, by something written in a paper, breaks a tension and a feeling that can never be put on paper at all.

And finally it was time to say good-bye on an evening in July. The weather had broken suddenly and the wind blew cold and gusty between the dispersal huts on the drome, raising dry clouds of sand. The Hurricanes were lined along the perimeter. The pilots were not very happy but they pretended to be very happy and the sergeant pilots fondled the busts of each other's Mae Wests and said heavy farewells.

There were many people there to say good-bye. We shook hands with everybody once and wished them luck, and then the take-off was delayed and we shook hands with everyone again. We all promised to write and knew that we should never keep the promises. Anderson addressed the pilots in language as if they were going to play football, and we all said good-bye once more. Then for the second time the take-off was delayed and the little Waafs who had at last begun to dry their tears began to cry all over again.

It was only when the take-off had begun at last that I realized that Auerbach was not there. Auerbach was going one way; the squadron another. Auerbach had not come to say good-bye. The Hurricanes flew once round the drome, in two flights of six, black against the grey evening sky, gradually formating. The little Waafs cried a little harder and the wind blew a little harder in a grey wave over the leaves of the potato patch beside the hut. I lifted my hand at last and drove away.

At the mess I found Auerbach alone. The ante-room was almost empty and there was no one laughing in the billiard-room.

'You didn't come,' I said to Auerbach.

'No.'

'You don't like good-byes,' I said.

'No.' He looked at me with the tender and now serious blue eyes that the newspapers had been vainly trying for weeks to describe. 'No, I do not like fuss,' he said. 'No fuss.'

I did not say anything. I walked away and into the garden. The grass and the leaves and the meadows under the hills were still green, but it was no longer the wonderful green of early summer. I walked across the grass and looked up at the empty sky and realized suddenly that something had gone.

All summer there had been something in the air. It was there no longer now.

THE BELL

WE DROVE ALONG the ferry road in the spring twilight and parked the car on the flat bank by the river, where the ferry bell hung on a sort of wooden gallows directly opposite the pub and a boat-landing by sallow-trees. I pulled the bell twice and the big sound donged over the water and the flat meadows and the fields of young corn beyond. The sallows were honey-cream with flower, and when finally the boy began to pull the ferry across to us I could see the yellow reflections of them pouring brokenly away behind the boat. In a few moments we were being ferried over.

In the bar of the pub we could look out of the windows, across the water, and see the ferry bell reflected, black and still, below the bare flat bank and the empty sky. I looked at it and it was like the old days again.

'Well, what will it be, sir?' Alf said. He flattened his hands on the bar.

'You don't remember me, Alf,' I said.

'Oh, I'm sorry!' Alf said. He looked at me, large grey eyes screwed up. 'I seem to remember your face. But I get so many Air Force boys in here.'

So I told him who I was. 'You remember,' I said. 'I used to come in a year or so back. With Mr. Taylor and Mr. Baker and Mr. Dibdin and Mr. Lockley. You remember.

The boys of the old squadron,' I said. 'You remember.'

'Well, bless my heart an' life,' Alf said. He wiped his right hand on his apron and held it across the bar.

'How are you, sir? How are you? Fancy me forgettin'.' He looked up at me with eyes large and tender with regret. We shook hands. 'But you know, sir, they come an' go. That's the truth. They come an' go.'

'Yes,' I said. 'They come and go.'

'Missus!' Alf shouted into the back of the bar. 'Come an' look who's here! Come on.'

And in a moment or two Mrs. Alf came into the bar. She was dressed in black. Her hair was the colour of the sallow-blooms by the landing-stage outside, and the flesh of her face hung in loose powdered folds on the high lace collar of her dress.

'There y'are,' Alf said. 'There's a gentleman I bet you don't remember.'

Mrs. Alf put her head on one side and smiled, pouting her scarlet lips.

'Don't talk so wet!' she said. 'Course I remember. Talk so wet. He's a friend of Mr. Lockley's.'

'Well!' Alf said. 'Well! If that don't call for one all round.'

'How de do,' Mrs. Alf said. 'How de do.' She held out her flabby white hand to me and smiled. The flesh of her hands was so thick that it had pressed the three rings on her marriage finger deep and tight, until they were like a small coiled gold spring locked on her fingers.

'How d'ye do,' I said. We shook hands, and I felt her hand over-soft and warm in mine.

'And this is Mr. Whitworth,' I said.

'How de do,' she said to my friend, and smiled.

'Well!' Alf said. 'Well!'

He had drawn four light ales, and now he set them on the bar. We took them up and held them for a moment in the air.

'Well! Here's to everybody!' Alf said.

'And here's to you,' I said.

'And here's to the boys of the old squadron,' Mrs. Alf said. 'God bless them.'

We drank and smiled at each other. Alf wiped his mouth with his hand and breathed hard. 'Ever see anything of the old squadron now, sir?'

'I saw Mr. Taylor the other day,' I said. 'Back from Canada. Mr. McIntyre, he's a prisoner.'

'No camp will hold him long,' Alf said.

'No,' I said. 'And Mr. Armstrong – you remember Maxie – he's an instructor. Mr. Butterworth, he's a squadron leader. Mr. Colton, he went back to Canada too.'

'Scattered all over the place,' Alf said.

'Yes,' I said. 'Mr. Feddington, he's with the Americans.'

'But there's something I wanted to ask you,' Mrs. Alf said. 'What happened to Mr. Lockley, sir? We never heard. What happened to Mr. Lockley?'

'He was a cough-drop,' Alf said.

'Oh, a nice boy!' Mrs. Alf said. 'You could always reckon on fun when Mr. Lockley was here.'

'You could an' all,' Alf said.

'Always up to some game. The number of glasses he broke in here is nobody's business. Always larkin' about. Never took nothing serious. Acrobats on the bar. Swimming the river at midnight. All the capers you could think of. I bet he never took nothing serious in his life, that boy.'

I did not say anything now.

'I tell you a thing he used to do,' Alf said, 'last thing at night I'd ferry him and the boys over. Shortest way home for 'em. I'd come back and lock the boat up. And then about a quarter of an hour later the bell would ring.'

'Mr. Lockley,' I said.

'Well, I ain't goin' to say it was and I ain't to say it wasn't,' Alf said. 'For whenever I got over there, after unlocking the boat an' everything, there was never anybody there. And that was him all over.'

'Yes,' I said.

'Him all over,' Alf said. 'I bet he never took nothing serious in his life. I bet he never took his flying serious. You couldn't imagine him. I bet he thought that was a lark.'

I put the glass down on the bar and looked at Alf, bit and heavy like a boxer, and Mrs. Alf, simple and florid, her rings coiled tight on her fingers.

'The trouble was he took it too seriously,' I said.

'Ah, go on,' Alf said.

'He never had any luck,' I said. I looked at the glass on the bar, and then up at Alf and his wife again. Their eyes were big with surprise and a sort of vacant tenderness as I began to tell them how it had been with Mr. Lockley. I began to tell them how, both in his personal life and his service life, Mr. Lockley had never had much luck: how he had lost his family in an air raid in London, how when he had come to the squadron he had never seemed to be able to land an aircraft as it should be landed, how little incidents and little accidents seemed to fill his life with a sort of haunting fatalism until he was almost afraid to fly. I told them how hard he tried; and how, the harder he tried, the worse it seemed to get for him. I told them how, through one of those unaccountable misjudgements, he landed a Halifax fifty feet off the runway and survived to face the problem of his own utter despair.

'Well, you wouldn't hardly credit it,' Alf said. 'You wouldn't hardly credit it.'

And finally I told them how, behind all the foolery and the larking and the tipsy lightheartedness and the practical joking, Lockley went out over Bremen and conquered at last the fears and failures and the accidents and incidents of despair.

'He rang the bell all right that night,' I said. 'His leg was smashed by flak but he didn't say anything. He went on and made one bombing run, and then another. His leg was very bad and the aircraft was falling to pieces. But he let all the crew get out, and then, at the very last, got out himself. He baled out with a smashed leg and they took him prisoner.'

There was silence in the bar as I finished speaking. I looked up at the eyes of Alf, big and stupid and friendly, and of Mrs. Alf, florid and kind-hearted and full of wonder. They were shining with unfallen tears.

'It just shows you, don't it?' Alf said.

'They gave him a medal for it,' I said.

'He earned it,' Alf said.

I looked at Mrs. Alf: tenderhearted behind all the powdered floridity, the lipstick cracked on her big lips, the tight rings on her too-fat fingers. 'He earned more than that,' she said.

A little later Alf himself ferried us back over the river. We shook hands and then at last drew slowly away along the river banks as Alf began to pull the ferry boat back towards the sallow-trees, glowing now like misty cream dust by the dark walls of the pub.

'Good night, sir,' Alf said. 'Nice to see you. Nice to hear about Mr. Lockley.'

'Good night, Alf,' we said. 'Good night.'

We drove away along the empty river bank. The water was dark and smooth in the falling light. We drove about a mile and then stopped before making the turn into the road. And as we stopped I could hear a sound coming up the way we had come, over the darkening water.

Someone was ringing the bell.

FREE CHOICE: FREE WORLD

THERE ARE NOT and never have been many Russian restaurants in England; but in a corner of a street in the town near the airfield the Koussevitskys have a little eating-place with marble-top tables and huge silver hand-stand cruets and yellow cane chairs and a smell of fried fish that is the shadow of Russia. Mrs. Koussevitsky is thin and olive-skinned. She has black-brown hair and large plum-black eyes, and when she speaks she lets fly with excited kindly hands. 'What you like? We gotta soup and hamburger and fried potatoes. Or you like fish? We got nice salmon wid cucumber salad. Is very nice.' And then: 'But oh! please God, when war is over I haff so nice food here, so nice – so nice, so nice, please God.'

When I first saw Mrs. Koussevitsky I could not guess her nationality. She might have been Italian. The subject, however, was a delicate one and I did not know how to approach it.

'You haven't lived long in England?' I said at last.

'Oh, no! oh, no! Where you think I from?'

'You might be from anywhere,' I said.

'Anywhere?'

'Well, you know,' I said, 'almost anywhere. From some little country somewhere. From some little country like Lithuania.'

163

'Lithuania?' she said. 'Lithuania?' She looked at me with wide still black eyes. 'How you know?'

'I don't know.'

'How you know I from Lithuania?' she said. 'How you know that? I was born in Lithuania! My brother is born in Lithuania! All my family is born there! How you know? How you know?'

I did not know at all how to account for that extraordinary piece of insight on my part.

'I just know,' I said.

'Oh, dear! oh, dear!' Mrs. Koussevitsky said, laughing and crying. 'Is wonderful! Oh, dear! oh, dear!'

From that moment Mrs. Koussevitsky took me to her heart. 'You come in Sunday and we have nice food. We have chicken and nice fish and beetroot soup.'

'Bortsh,' I said.

'Bortsh, yes! How you know?'

'Everybody knows bortsh,' I said. 'Bortsh is Russia. Roast beef is England.'

'Oi! Oi!' she said, half crying, half laughing again. 'Oi! Oi!' she called back in a loud excited voice into the kitchen behind the restaurant. 'Here is a gentleman who like bortsh! You hear!'

'Oi! Oi!' Mr. Koussevitsky called. 'I hear!'

After that I became, to the Koussevitskys, the man who liked bortsh. Whenever I went there Mrs. Koussevitsky came into the restaurant wiping her hands in her apron and then throwing them excitedly up into the air and clasping them together. 'Oi!' she would call, 'here is the young man from the Air Force! The young man who likes bortsh! You hear!'

'Oi,' Mr. Koussevitsky would call. 'I hear.'

But somehow, although I was always the young man who liked bortsh and although Mrs. Koussevitsky always said there would be bortsh on Sunday, there never was any bortsh.

Either there were no beetroots or the bortsh had all been eaten or Mrs. Koussevitsky had decided to make something else after all. Similarly there was never any chicken; the salmon was always gone; and it was the wrong time of the year for cucumber. And so after a time, faced with nothing but the usual sausage and fried potatoes, I began to feel, as we say, that I had had it with the Koussevitskys.

Then one day Mrs. Koussevitsky asked me a question.

'You know Mr. Markus?' she said.

'No, I didn't know him. I know all about him,' I said.

'All about him?' she said. 'All about him? Then where is he? Where is he now? He used to come in here. Now he doesn't come.'

'No,' I said.

'Well, why doesn't he come? Isn't he on the station any more? Where is he?'

'We don't know,' I said. 'His Spitfire was lost in the attack on the *Scharnhorst*.'

Mrs. Koussevitsky was very quiet, holding her hands.

'He was Lithuanian,' she said.

'Yes,' I said, 'the only Lithuanian.'

'He was so nice man. I don't believe nice men like that are killed. I don't believe that nice Mr. Markus was killed!' she said. 'I don't believe it.'

I did not say anything. It is the thing they all say; the thing they all believe. In the eyes of those who love them, pilots are never dead. So when Mrs. Koussevitsky said, 'I believe that nice Mr. Markus is all right,' I thought it kinder not to speak.

After that, whenever I went into the Koussevitskys we talked about Mr. Markus. There were things about him that Mrs. Koussevitsky did not know, and I told her them. There were things about him I did not know, and Mrs. Koussevitsky told them to me. I told her how he was the only Lithuanian in the Air Force; a man from a country not at war. I told her how he had played international football and what a distinguished, important, diplomatic sort of flyer he had been before the war in his own country, how he had flown important personages all over Europe and how he had been decorated in every capital, until his tunic looked like a coat of many colours. She told me in turn how he used to come into the restaurant with a young lady and eat the Koussevitskys' simple food, and talk, as exiles always talk, of their own country. I told her how he had flown since he was a schoolboy; and how, when the war which was not his began, he had gone to France to fly for France; and then how, after France fell, he had come to England to fly for us. I told her what an engaging, temperamental person he was, and she told me over and over again how she could not believe he had been killed.

We talked of him so often, she asking me again and again for news and I telling her and really knowing that there was no more news to tell, that I began to see the Koussevitskys' little restaurant, with its sausages and fried potatoes, and its bortsh that I never tasted, as a corner of Lithuania in England. I was sure that Markus was dead; Mrs. Koussevitsky was sure that he was living. Whichever way it was I used to get considerable satisfaction from the very fact that Markus had been with us at all: that as a free man, making a free choice, entering a war that he had no need to enter, he had made the choice he had.

But if I had great satisfaction in Markus, Mrs. Koussevitsky had greater faith. And finally one day I was able to go down to Koussevitskys' and see that faith justified.

'I have come to tell you something,' I said. 'Mr. Markus is all right.'

'Is – is what? – is *all right*?' she said. 'Is *all right*?'

'He is a prisoner,' I said. 'It has just come through.'

Now it was Mrs. Koussevitsky who could not speak. She stood crying quietly, slowly clasping and unclasping her hands. Whether she was crying for Markus or Lithuania or Russia or simply out of joy I could not tell. It was her great moment and she was very proud. I felt a great satisfaction too. I remembered the last anyone had ever seen of Markus: how he had taken the Spitfire down to nought feet over the *Scharnhorst* and had put her practically down the funnels and was never seen again. It was a great satisfaction to know that he had performed a miracle and was alive.

'Oh, please God!' Mrs. Koussevitsky said, 'when war is over we will have bigga celebration! So big, so nice! So nice food! So nice, so nice, so nice, please God.'

And, please God, we will.

Sergeant Carmichael

I

FOR SOME TIME he had had a feeling that none of them knew where they were going. They had flown over France without seeing the land. Now they were flying in heavy rain without a glimpse of the sea. He was very young, just twenty, and suddenly he had an uneasy idea that they would never see either the land or the sea again.

'Transmitter pretty u.s., sir,' he said.

For a moment there was no answer. Then Davidson, the captain, answered automatically, 'Keep trying, Johnny,' and he answered 'O.K.,' quite well knowing there was nothing more he could do. He sat staring straight before him. Momentarily he was no longer part of the aircraft. He was borne away from it on sound-waves of motors and wind and rain, and for a few minutes he was back in England, recalling and reliving odd moments of life there. He recalled for a second or two his first day on the station; it was August and he remembered that some straw had blown in from the fields across the runways and that the wind of the take-offs whirled it madly upward, yellow and shining in the sun. He recalled his father eating redcurrants in the garden that same summer and how the crimson juice had spurted on to his moustache,

169

so that he looked rather ferocious every time he said, 'That, if you want it, is my opinion.' And then he remembered, most curiously of all, a girl in a biscuit-yellow hat sitting in a deck-chair on the seafront, eating a biscuit-yellow ice-cream, and how he had been fascinated because hat and ice were miraculously identical in colour and how he had wanted to ask her, with nervous bravado because he was very young, if she bought her hats to match her ice-cream or her ice-cream to match her hats, but how he never did. He did not know why he recalled these moments, clear as glass, except perhaps that they were moments of a life he was never going to see again.

He was suddenly ejected out of this past world, fully alert and aware that they were not flying straight. They had not been flying straight for some time. They were stooging round and round, bumping heavily, and losing height. He sat very tense, and became gradually aware that this tension was part of the 'plane. It existed in each one of them from Davidson and Porter in the nose, down through Johnson and Hargreaves and himself to Carmichael, in the tail.

He heard Davidson's voice. 'How long since we had contact with base?'

He looked at his watch; it was almost midnight. 'A little under an hour and three-quarters,' he said.

Again there was silence; and again he felt the tension running through the 'plane. He was aware of their chances and almost aware, now, of what Davidson was going to say.

'One more try, boys. Sing out if you see anything. If not it's down in the drink.'

He sat very still. They were losing a little height. His stomach felt sour and he remembered that he could not swim.

For some reason he never thought of it again. His thoughts were scattered by Davidson's voice.

'Does anyone see what I see? Isn't that a light? About two points to starboard.'

He looked out; there was nothing he could see.

'I'm going down to have a look-see,' Davidson said. 'It *is* a light.'

As they were going down he looked out again, but again he could see nothing. Then he heard Davidson speaking to Carmichael.

'Hack the fuselage door off, Joe. This looks like a light-ship. If it is we're as good as home. Tell me when you're ready and I'll put her down.'

He sat very still, hearing the sound of hatchet blows as Carmichael struck at the fuselage. He felt suddenly colder, and then knew that it must be because Carmichael had finished and that there was a gap where the door had been. He heard again the deep slow Canadian accent of Carmichael's voice, saying, 'O.K., skipper, all set,' and then the remote flat English voice of Davidson in reply:

'All right, get the dinghy ready. All three of you. Get ready and heave it out when I put her down.'

Helping Joe and Hargreaves and Johnson with the dinghy he was no longer aware of fear. He was slung sideways across the aircraft. There was not much room. The dinghy seemed very large and he wondered how they would get it out. This troubled him until he felt the 'plane roaring down in the darkness, and it continued to trouble him for a second after the 'plane had hit the water with a great crash that knocked him back against the fuselage. He did not remember getting up. Something was wrong with his left wrist, and he thought of his watch. It was a good watch, a navigational watch, given him by his father on a birthday. The next moment he knew that the dinghy had gone and he knew that he had helped, somehow, to push it out. Carmichael had also gone. The sea was rocking the aircraft violently to and fro, breaking water against his knees and feet. A second later he stretched out his hand and felt nothing before him but the open space in the fuselage where the door had been.

He knew then that it must be his turn to go. He heard Carmichael's voice calling from what seemed a great distance out of the darkness and the rain. He did not know what he was calling. It was all confused, he did not answer, but a second later he stretched out his hands blindly and went down on his belly in the sea.

II

When he came up again it was to find himself thinking of the girl in the biscuit-coloured hat and how much, that day, he had liked the sea, opaque and green and smooth as the pieces of sea-washed glass he had picked up on the shore. It flashed through his mind that this was part of the final imagery that comes with drowning, and he struggled wildly to keep his face above water. He could hear again the voice of Carmichael, shouting, but the shock of sea-water struck like ice on his breast and throat, so that he could not shout in answer. The sea was very rough. It heaved him upwards and then down again with sweeps of slow and violent motion. It tossed him about in this way until he realized at last that these slow, barbaric waves were really keeping him up, that the Mae West was working and that he was sinking away no longer.

From the constancy of Carmichael's shouts he felt that Carmichael must have seized, and was probably on, the dinghy. But he was not prepared for the shout: 'She's upside down!' and then a moment or two later two voices, yelling his name.

'Johnny! Can you hear us? Can you hear us now?'

He let out a great yell in answer but sea-water broke down his throat, for a moment suffocated him, bearing him down and under the trough of a wave. He came up sick and struggling, spitting water, frightened. His boots were very heavy now under the water and it seemed as if he were being sucked continually down. He tried to wave his arms above his head but one arm had no response. It filled him suddenly with violent pain.

'O.K., Johnny, O.K., O.K.,' Carmichael said.

He could not speak. He knew that his arm was broken. He felt Carmichael's hands painfully clutching his one free hand. He remembered for no reason at all that Carmichael had been a pitcher for a baseball team in Montreal, and he felt the hands move down until they clutched his wrist, holding him so strongly that it was almost a pain.

'Can you bear up?' Carmichael said. 'Johnny, try bearing up. It's O.K., Johnny. We're here, on the dinghy. Hargreaves is here. Johnson's here. We're all here except the skipper. It's O.K., Johnny. Can you heave? Where's your other arm?'

'I think it's bust,' he said.

He tried heaving himself upward. He tried again, helped by Carmichael's hands, but something each time drew the dinghy away. He tried again and then again. Each time the same thing happened, and once or twice the sea, breaking on the dinghy, hit him in the face, blinding him.

He knew suddenly what was wrong. It was not only his arm but his belt. Each time he heaved upward the belt caught under the dinghy and pushed it away. In spite of knowing it he heaved again and all at once felt very tired, feeling that only Carmichael's hands were between this tiredness and instant surrender. This painful heaving and sudden tiredness were repeated. They went on for some time. He heard Carmichael's voice continually and once or twice the sea hit him again, blinding him, and once, blinded badly, he wanted to wipe his face with his hands.

Suddenly Carmichael was talking again. 'Can you hang on? If I can get my knee on something I'll get leverage. I'll pull you up. Can you hang on?'

Before he could answer the sea hit him again. The waves seemed to split his contact with Carmichael. It momentarily cut away his hands. For an instant it was as if he were in a bad and terrifying dream, falling through space.

Then Carmichael was holding him again. 'I got you now, Johnny. I'm kneeling on Dicky. Your belt ought to clear now. If you try hard it ought to clear first time.'

The sea swung him away. As he came back the belt did not hit the dinghy so violently. He was kept almost clear. Then the sea swung him away again. On this sudden wave of buoyancy he realized that it was now, or perhaps never, that he must pull himself back. He clenched his hand violently; and then suddenly before he was ready, and very lightly as if he were a child, the force of the new wave and the strength of Carmichael's hands threw him on the dinghy, face down.

He wanted to lie there for a long time. He lay for only a second, and then got up. He felt the water heaving in his boots and the salt sickness of it in his stomach. He did not feel at all calm but was terrified for an instant by the shock of being safe.

'There was a light,' he said. 'That's why he came down here. That's why he came down. There was a light.'

He looked around at the sea as he spoke. Sea and darkness were one, unbroken except where waves struck the edge of the dinghy with spits of faintly phosphorescent foam. It had ceased raining now but the wind was very strong and cold, and up above lay the old unbroken ten-tenths cloud. There was not even a star that could have been mistaken for a light. He knew that perhaps there never had been.

He went into a slight stupor brought on by pain and the icy sea-water. He came out of it to find himself furiously baling water from the dinghy with one hand. He noticed that the rest were baling with their caps. He had lost his cap. His one hand made a nerveless cup that might have been stone for all the feeling that was in it now.

The sea had a rhythmical and awful surge that threw the dinghy too lightly up the glassy arcs of oncoming waves and then too steeply over the crest into the trough beyond. Each time they came down into a trough the dinghy shipped a lot of water. Each time they baled frenziedly, sometimes throwing the water over each other. His good hand remained dead. He still did not feel the water with it but he felt it on his face, sharp as if the spray were splintered and frozen glass. Then whenever they came to the crest of a wave there was a split second when they could look for a light. 'Hell, there should be a light,' he thought. 'He saw one. He shouted it out. That's why he came down,' but each time the sea beyond the crest of the new wave remained utterly dark as before.

'What the hell,' he said. 'There should be a light! There *was* a light.'

'All right, kid,' Carmichael said. 'There'll be one.'

He knew then that he was excited. He tried not to be excited. For a long time he didn't speak, but his mind remained excited. He felt drunk with the motion of pain and the water and sick with the saltness of the water. There were moments when he ceased baling and held his one hand strengthlessly at his side, tired out, wanting to give up. He did not know how he kept going after a time or how they kept the water from swamping the dinghy.

Coming out of periods of stupor, he would hear

Carmichael talking. The deep Canadian voice was slow and steady. It attracted him. He found himself listening simply to the sound and the steadiness of it, regardless of words. It had the quality of Carmichael's hands; it was calm and steadfast.

It occurred to him soon that the voice had another quality. It was like the baling of the water; it never stopped. He heard Carmichael talking of ball games in Montreal; the way the crowd ragged you and how you took no notice and how it was all part of the game; and then how he was injured in the game one summer and for two months couldn't play and how he went up into Quebec province for the fishing. It was hot weather and he would fish mostly in the late evenings, often by moonlight. The lake trout were big and strong and sometimes a fish took you an hour to get in. Sometimes at week-ends he went back to Quebec and he would eat steaks as thick, he said, as a volume of Dickens and rich with onions and butter. They were lovely with cold light beer, and the whole thing set you back about two dollars and a half.

'Good eh, Johnny?' he would say. 'You ought to come over there some day.'

All the time they baled furiously. There was no break in the clouds and the wind was so strong that it sometimes swivelled the dinghy round like a toy.

How long this went on he did not know. But a long time later Carmichael suddenly stopped talking and then as suddenly began again.

'Hey, Johnny boy, there's your light!'

He was startled and he looked up wildly, not seeing anything.

'Not that way, boy. Back of you. Over there.'

He turned his head stiffly. There behind him he could see the dim cream edge of daylight above the line of the sea.

'That's the light we want,' Carmichael said. 'It don't go out in a hurry either.'

The colour of daylight was deeper, like pale butter, when he looked over his shoulder again. He remembered then that it was late summer. He thought that now, perhaps it would be three o'clock.

As the daylight grew stronger, changing from cream and yellow to a cool grey bronze, he saw for the first time the barbaric quality of the sea. He saw the faces of Carmichael and Hargreaves and Johnson. They were grey-yellow with weariness and touched at the lips and ears and under the eyes with blue.

He was very thirsty. He could feel a thin caking of salt on his lips. He tried to lick his lips with his tongue but it was very painful. There was no moisture on his tongue and only the taste of salt, very harsh and bitter, in his mouth. His arm was swollen and he was sick with pain.

'Take it easy a minute, kid,' Carmichael said. 'We'll bale in turns. You watch out for a ship or a kite or anything you can see. I'll tell you when it's your turn.'

He sat on the edge of the dinghy and stared at the horizon and the sky. Both were empty. He rubbed the salt out of his eyes and then closed them for a moment, worn out.

'Watch out,' Carmichael said. 'We're in the Channel. We know that. There should be ships and there should be aircraft. Keep watching.'

He kept watching. His eyes were painful with salt and only half-open. Now and then the sea hit the dinghy and broke right over it, but he did not care. For some reason he did not think of listening, but suddenly he shut his eyes and after a moment or two he heard a sound. It was rather like the sound of the sea beating gently on sand, and he remembered again the day when he had seen the girl in the biscuit-coloured hat and how it was summer and how much he had liked the sea. That day the sea had beaten on the shore with the same low sound.

As the sound increased he suddenly opened his eyes. He felt for a moment that he was crazy, and then he began shouting.

'It's a 'plane! It's a bloody 'plane! It's a 'plane, I tell you, it's a 'plane!'

'Sit down,' Carmichael said.

The dinghy was rocking violently. The faces of all four men were upturned, grey-yellow in the stronger light.

'There she is!' he shouted. 'There she is!'

The 'plane was coming over from the north-east, at about five thousand. He began to wave his hands. She seemed to be coming straight above them. Hargreaves and Johnson and then Carmichael also began to wave. They all waved frantically and Hargreaves shouted, 'It's a Hudson, boys. Wave like raving Hallelujah! It's a Hudson.'

The 'plane came over quite fast and very steady, flying straight. It looked the colour of iron except for the bright rings of the markings in the dull sea-light of the early morning. It flew on quite straight and they were still waving frantically with their hands and caps long after it had ceased looking like a far-off gull in the sky.

He came out of the shock of this disappointment to realize that Carmichael was holding him in the dinghy with one arm.

'I'm all right,' he said.

'I know,' Carmichael said.

He knew then that he was not all right. He felt dizzy. A slow river of cold sweat seemed to be pouring from his hair down his backbone.

'What happened?' he said.

'You're all right,' Carmichael said. 'Don't try to stand up

again, that's all. How's your arm? I wish there was something I could do.'

'It's O.K.,' he said.

He remembered the 'plane. The sky was now quite light, barred with warm strips of orange low above the water in the east. He remembered also that it was summer. The wind was still strong and cold but soon, he thought, there will be sun. He looked overhead at the grey-blue and the yellow-orange bars of cloud. They were breaking a little more overhead and he knew now that it would be a fair day for flying.

'Does the sun rise in the east or a little to the north-east?' Carmichael said.

They held a little discussion, and Johnny and Hargreaves agreed that in summer it rose a little to the north-east.

'In that case we seem to be drifting almost due north. If the wind helps us we might drift into the coast. It's still strong.'

'It's about forty,' Hargreaves said. 'It must have been about eighty last night.'

'It was a point or two west of south then,' Johnny said.

'I think it's still there,' Carmichael said.

They all spoke rather slowly. His own lips felt huge and dry with blisters. It was painful for him to speak. He was not hungry, but the back of his throat was scorched and raw with salt. His tongue was thick and hot and he wanted to roll it out of his mouth, so that it would get sweet and cool in the wind.

'Keep your mouth shut, Johnny,' Carmichael said. 'Keep it shut.'

He discovered that Carmichael was still holding him by the arm. In the hour or two that went by between the dis-appearance of the Hudson and the time when the sun was well up and he could feel the warmth of it on his face he continually wanted to protest; to tell Carmichael that he was all right. Yet he never did and all the time Carmichael held him and he was glad.

All the time they watched the sea and the sky and most of the time Carmichael talked to them. He talked to them again of Canada, the lakes in the summertime, the fishing, the places where you could eat in Montreal. The sea was less violent now, but the waves, long and low and metallically glittering in the sun, swung the dinghy ceaselessly up and down troughs that bristled with destructive edges of foam. Towards the middle of the morning Hargreaves was very sick. He leaned his head forward on his knees and sat very quiet for a long time, too weak to lift his head. The sickness itself became covered and churned and finally washed away by incoming water. After this only Johnson and Carmichael troubled to watch the horizon, and they took turns at baling the water, Carmichael using one hand.

For some time none of them spoke. Finally when Johnny looked up again it was to see that Johnson too had closed his eyes against the glitter of sunlight and that only Carmichael was watching the sea. He was watching in a curious attitude. As he held Johnny with one hand he would lean forward and with his hat bale a little water out of the dinghy. Then he would transfer the hat from one hand to the other and with the free hand press the fabric of the dinghy as you press the inner tube of a tyre. As he pressed it seemed flabby. Then he would look up and gaze for a few moments at the horizon, northwards, where at intervals the sea seemed to crystallize into long lips of misty grey. For a long time Johnny sat watching him, following the movements of his hands and the arrested progress of his eyes.

Very slowly he realized what was happening. He did not move. He wanted to speak but the back of his throat was raw and his tongue was thick and inflexible. When he suddenly

180

opened his mouth his lips split and there was blood in the cracks that was bitterly salt as he licked it with his tongue.

He did not know which struck him first: the realization that the thin lips of grey on the horizon were land or that the dinghy was losing air. For a second or two his emotions were cancelled out. The dinghy was upside down; the bellows were gone. He felt slightly light-headed. Above the horizon the clouds were white-edged now, and suddenly the sun broke down through them and shone on the line of land, turning the lips of grey to brown. He knew then that it was land. There could be no mistake. But looking down suddenly into the dinghy he knew that there was and could be no mistake there either.

He began to shout. He did not know what he shouted. His mouth was very painful. He rocked his body forward and began to bale excitedly with his free hand. In a moment the rest were shouting too.

'Steady,' Carmichael said, 'steady.'

'How far is it away?' Hargreaves said. 'Five miles? Five or six?'

'Nearer ten.'

'I'll take a bet.'

'You'd better take one on the air in the dinghy.'

It was clear that Hargreaves did not know about the air in the dinghy. He ceased baling and sat very tense. His tongue was thick and grey-pink and hanging out of his mouth.

It seemed to Johnny that the dinghy, slowly losing resilience, was like something dying underneath them.

'Now don't anybody go and get excited,' Carmichael said. 'We must be drifting in fast, and if we drift in far enough and she gives out we can swim. You all better bale now while you can. All right, Johnny? Can you bale?'

Baling frantically with his one hand, looking up at intervals at the horizon, now like a thin strip of cream-brown paint squeezed along the edge of the sea, he tried not to think of the fact that he could not swim.

All the time he felt the dinghy losing air. He felt its flabbiness grow in proportion to his own weight. It moved very heavily and sluggishly in the troughs of water, and waves broke over it more often now. Sometimes the water rose almost to the knees of the men. He could not feel his feet and several times it seemed as if the bottom of the dinghy had fallen out and that beneath him there was nothing but the bottom of the sea.

It went on like this for a long time, the dinghy losing air, the land coming a little nearer, deeper-coloured now, with veins of green.

'God, we'll never make it,' Hargreaves said. 'We'll never make it.'

Carmichael did not speak. The edge of the dinghy was low against the water, almost level. The sea lapped over it constantly and it was more now than they could bale.

Johnny looked at the land. The sun was shining down on smooth uplands of green and calm brown squares of upturned earth. Below lay long chalk cliffs, changing from sea-grey to white in the sun. He felt suddenly exhausted and desperate. He felt that he hated the sea. He was frightened of it and suddenly lost his head and began to bale with one arm, throwing the water madly everywhere.

'We'll never do it!' he shouted. 'We'll never do it. Why the hell didn't that Hudson see us! What the hell do they do in those fancy kites!'

'Shut up,' Carmichael said.

He felt suddenly quiet and frightened.

'Shut up. She's too heavy, that's all. Take your boots off.'

Hargreaves and Johnson stopped baling and took off their boots. He tried to take off his own boots but they seemed part of his feet and with only one arm he was too weak to pull them off. Then Carmichael took off his own boots. He took off his socks too, and Johnny could see that Carmichael's feet were blue and dead.

For a minute he could not quite believe what he saw next. He saw Carmichael roll over the side of the dinghy into the sea. He went under and came up again at once, shaking the water from his hair. 'O.K.,' he shouted, 'O.K. Keep baling. I'm pushing her in. She'll be lighter now.'

Carmichael put his hands on the end of the dinghy and swam with his feet.

'I'm coming over too,' Hargreaves said.

'No. Keep baling. Keep her light. There'll be time to come over.'

They went on like this for some time. The situation in the dinghy was bad, but he did not think of it. His knees were sometimes wholly submerged and the dinghy was flabby and without life. All the time he hated the sea and kept his eyes in desperation on the shore. Then Carmichael gave Hargreaves the order to go over and Hargreaves rolled over the side as Carmichael had done and came up soon and began swimming in the same way.

They were then about five hundred yards from the shore and he could see sheep in the fields above the cliffs, but no houses. The land looked washed and bright and for some reason abandoned, as if no one had ever set foot there. The sea was calm now, but it still washed over the dinghy too fast for him to bale and he still hated it. Then suddenly Johnson went over the side without waiting for a word from Carmichael, and he was alone in the dinghy, being pushed along by the three men. But he knew soon that it could not last. The dinghy was almost flat, and between the force of the three men pushing and the resistance of water it crumpled and submerged and would not move.

As if there were something funny about this Johnson began laughing. He himself felt foolish and scared and waited with clenched teeth for the dinghy to go down.

It went down before he was ready, throwing him backwards. He felt a wave hit him and then he went under, his boots dragging him down. He struggled violently and quite suddenly saw the sky. His arm was very painful and he felt lop-sided. He was lying on his back and he knew that he was moving, not of his own volition but easily and strongly, looking at the lakes of summer sky between the white and indigo hills of cloud. He was uneasy and glad at the same time. The sea still swamped over his face, scorching his broken lips, but he was glad because he knew that Carmichael was holding him again and taking him in to shore.

What seemed a long time later he knew that they were very near the shore. He heard the loud warm sound of breaking waves. He was borne forward in long surges of the tide. At last he could no longer feel Carmichael's arms, but tired and kept up by his Mae West, he drifted in of his own accord. The sun was strong on his face and he thought suddenly of the things he had thought about in the 'plane: the straw on the runways, his father eating the currants, the girl in the biscuit-coloured hat. He felt suddenly that they were the things for which he had struggled. They were his life. The waves took him gradually farther and farther up the shore, until his knees beat on the sand. He saw Carmichael and Johnson and Hargreaves waiting on the shore. At last new waves took him far up the shore until he lay still on the wet slope of sand and his arms were outstretched to the sky.

As he lay there the sea ran down over his body and receded away. It was warm and gentle on his hands and he was afraid of it no longer.

THE HISTORY OF VINTAGE

The famous American publisher Alfred A. Knopf (1892–1984) founded Vintage Books in the United States in 1954 as a paperback home for the authors published by his company. Vintage was launched in the United Kingdom in 1990 and works independently from the American imprint although both are part of the international publishing group, Random House.

Vintage in the United Kingdom was initially created to publish paperback editions of books bought by the prestigious literary hardback imprints in the Random House Group such as Jonathan Cape, Chatto & Windus, Hutchinson and later William Heinemann, Secker & Warburg and The Harvill Press. There are many Booker and Nobel Prize-winning authors on the Vintage list and the imprint publishes a huge variety of fiction and non-fiction. Over the years Vintage has expanded and the list now includes great authors of the past – who are published under the Vintage Classics imprint – as well as many of the most influential authors of the present. In 2012 Vintage Children's Classics was launched to include the much-loved authors of our youth.

For a full list of the books Vintage publishes,
please visit our website
www.vintage-books.co.uk

For book details and other information about the classic authors we publish, please visit the Vintage Classics website
www.vintage-classics.info